Upper Fourth

This is th[...]
in the Malory Towers series

This Armada book belongs to:

Enid Blyton

Upper Fourth at Malory Towers

ARMADA

First published in the UK in 1949
by Methuen & Co. Ltd
Republished by Dragon Books in 1967
First published in Armada in 1988
This impression 1990

Armada is an imprint of
the Children's Division, part of
the Harper Collins Publishing Group,
8 Grafton Street, London W1X 3LA

Printed and bound in Great Britain by
William Collins Sons & Co. Ltd, Glasgow

Darrell goes back to School with Felicity

Darrell Rivers was very excited. It was the day to
return to Malory Towers, her boarding school – and
this time she was taking her young sister Felicity with
her.

Felicity stood on the front steps beside her fifteen-
year-old sister, dressed in the same brown and orange
uniform, feeling excited, too. She was almost thirteen,
and should have gone to Malory Towers two terms
before, but she had been ill and had to stay at home.

Now it was the summer term, and she was to go
with Darrell at last. She had heard so much about her
sister's school – the fun they had there, the classrooms
overlooking the sea, the four towers in which the two
hundred and fifty girls slept, the great swimming pool
hollowed out of the rocks on the shore . . . there was
no end to the things that Darrell had told her.

"It's a good thing we're going by train this time,
not by car," said Darrell. "You'll travel down with
the girls then, and get to know some of them. Sally's
going by train, too."

Sally was Darrell's best friend, and had been ever
since her first term at Malory Towers almost four years
ago.

"I hope I get a friend like Sally," said Felicity,
nervously. "I'm shyer than you, Darrell. I'm sure
I shall never pluck up enough courage to speak to
anyone! And if Miss Potts gets cross with me I shall
sink through the floor!"

Miss Potts was the first-form mistress, and also the house mistress for North Tower, the tower to which Darrell belonged, and to which her young sister would go, too.

"Oh, you needn't be afraid of Potty," said Darrell, with a laugh, quite forgetting how scared *she* had been of her when she was in the first form. "Dear old Potty – she's a good sort."

Their father's car drew up at the front door, and the two girls ran down the steps. Mr Rivers looked at them and smiled.

"*Both* off this time!" he said. "Well, I remember quite well Darrell going off alone for the first time almost four years ago. She was twelve then – now you're fifteen, aren't you, Darrell!"

"Yes," said Darrell, getting into the car with Felicity. "And I remember you saying to me, 'you'll get a lot out of Malory Towers – see that you put a lot back!' "

"Daddy's said that to me, too," said Felicity. "I'm jolly lucky to have an older sister to show me round – though honestly I feel as if I know every corner of Malory Towers already."

"Now, where's Mother?" said her father, and he hooted the horn. "Really, this is a dreadful family to collect. If your mother appears in good time, one of you girls is missing, and if you girls are here, your mother is not! We shall miss the train if we don't look out!"

Usually they went all the way down to Cornwall to Malory Towers by car, but this time it was impossible, so Mr Rivers was driving them up to London and seeing them off on the school train. Felicity had sometimes been to see her sister off by train, and had felt scared of all the girls chattering and laughing on the platform – now this time she was actually going to be one of them! She hugged her tennis racket to herself and thought joyfully of the coming term.

Mrs Rivers came running down the steps, looking very pretty in a simple grey suit with a little blue blouse. Darrell and Felicity looked at her proudly. Parents mattered a lot when you were at boarding school! Everyone wanted to be proud of the way their fathers and mothers looked and spoke and behaved. It was dreadful if a mother came in a silly hat, or if a father came looking very untidy.

"My dear, we were *just* going without you," said Mr Rivers. "Now – have we really got everything? Last time we got five miles on the way and then you said you'd forgotten Darrell's night case."

"Yes, we've got everything, Daddy," said Darrell. "I've checked every single thing – night cases, with brush and comb, toothbrush and paste, night things, health certificate, everything! Tennis rackets to carry, and bowler hats for riding! We can't pack those, they're too awkward."

Felicity glanced round to see if her new bowler hat was there, too. She felt very proud of it. She had only had a jockey cap before.

They set off in the car to drive to London. Felicity's heart sank a little as her home disappeared from view. Three whole months before she would see it again! Then she cheered up as Darrell began chatting about the girls.

"I hope Bill will arrive with all her seven brothers on horseback," she said. "It's such a sight to see them all galloping up the school drive. Bill was supposed to come in her parents' car the first term she came, but she slipped off, got her horse, Thunder, and came with all her brothers on their horses, too!"

"Bill's real name is Wilhemina, isn't it?" said Felicity, remembering. "Do even the mistresses call her

Bill?"

"Some of them," said Darrell. "Not the head, of course. And Miss Williams, our fourth-form mistress, doesn't either. She's a bit starchy – very prim and proper, but I like her now. I didn't at first."

It didn't seem long before they were all on the station platform, finding their way between hosts of excited girls to a North Tower carriage. Felicity felt shy and nervous. Oh, dear – so many girls, and they all knew one another, and she didn't know anyone. Oh, yes she did – there was Sally, Darrell's friend, coming towards her, smiling.

"Hallo, Darrell, hallo, Felicity – so you're really coming to Malory Towers at last. Jolly good! Wish I was coming for the first time, too, so that I would have years and years of it in front of me, like you. You don't know how lucky you are!"

"I remember someone saying that to *me* on my first day," said Darrell. "I was twelve then – now I'm going on for sixteen. Gosh, how old!"

"Yes – and don't forget we'll feel jolly old before this term's out!" said a familiar voice behind Darrell. "We've all got to work for School Certificate! My hair will be quite grey by the end of term!"

"Hallo, Alicia!" said Darrell, warmly. "Did you have good hols? Look, this is my young sister, Felicity. She's a new girl this term."

"Is she really?" said Alicia. "Well, I must find my cousin then. She's a new girl this term, too. Now where is she? I've lost her twice already!"

She disappeared, and Sally and Darrell laughed. They were sure that Alicia wouldn't bother much about any new-girl cousin! However, she appeared again almost at once bringing with her a twelve-year-old girl, very like her.

"This is June," she said. "You might as well make

8

friends with Felicity, June, because you'll see plenty of her this term and for a good many years to come! Though whether Felicity will *want* to see much of you after she knows you well is very doubtful."

Darrell looked at Alicia to see whether she meant this or not. You never knew with sharp-tongued Alicia! June looked all right, and had a very determined chin and mouth. A bit domineering, Darrell thought – but being in the bottom form of the school didn't give you much chance for that kind of thing. The older girls just sat on you hard if you didn't keep your place.

"Look!" said Alicia, nudging Darrell and Sally. "There's Gwendoline Mary – come by train instead of car – and staging the same old scene as ever!"

Felicity and June turned to see. They saw a fair-haired girl with large, pale blue eyes, saying goodbye to her mother and her old governess. It was a very sentimental farewell, and a lot of sniffing was going on.

"Gwendoline always does that," said Alicia in disgust. "At her age, too! You can forgive a first-former going away from home for the first time – but a fifteen-year-old, no!"

"Well, it doesn't last long," said Sally. "Gwendoline won't even bother to remember to wave to her mother, I'm sure, once she gets into the carriage."

Sally's mother was talking to Darrell's parents. There were no tears or protestations there! Darrell was thankful that her mother and father were so sensible. She looked at Felicity, and was pleased to see her young sister looking interested and happy.

More girls came up and surrounded Darrell and the others. "Hallo! Had good hols? I say, is this your young sister? Has she got a temper like yours, Darrell?"

This was from Irene, harum-scarum as usual, her

night case coming undone, and her coat lacking a button already.

"Well – Felicity *has* got a temper," said Darrell, with a laugh. "All our family have. I don't expect Felicity will show hers much though. She'll be too shy her first term."

"I don't know about that!" said Sally, slyly. "I seem to remember *you* going off the deep end properly in your first term, Darrell! Who sent me flying to the ground that first half term – and who gave dear Gwendoline some very hearty slaps in the swimming pool?"

"Oh, dear – yes, I was dreadful," said Darrell, and she blushed. "Really awful. I'm sure Felicity will never do anything like that."

"My cousin's got a bit of a temper, too," said Alicia, with a grin. "She's only got brothers, and you should hear them shout and yell at one another when they disagree."

"Here's Miss Potts," said Sally, as the first-form mistress came up with a list in her hand. "Hallo, Miss Potts, have you collected everyone?"

"Yes, I think so," said Miss Potts, "except Irene. Oh there you are, Irene. I suppose it didn't occur to you to come and report your arrival to me? Thank goodness Belinda is going by car. That's one less scatterbrain to see to. Now, you'd better get into your carriages. There are only four more minutes to go."

There was a scramble into the carriages. Sally and Darrell pulled Felicity into theirs. "The new girls are supposed to go with Potty in her carriage," said Darrell, "but we'll let you come in ours. Goodbye, Mother, goodbye, Daddy! We'll write on Sunday and tell you all the news."

"Goodbye!" said Felicity, in rather a small voice. "Thanks for lovely hols."

10

"Thank goodness we haven't got Gwendoline in our carriage," said Alicia. "We are at least spared the history of all her uninteresting family, and what happened to them last hols. Even her dogs are uninteresting!"

Everyone laughed. The guard blew his whistle. Doors slammed, and the train then moved off slowly. Parents and girls waved madly. Darrell sank back into her seat.

"Off to Malory Towers again!" she said, joyfully. "Good old Malory Towers!"

Everybody's Back Again!

The journey was a very long one, but the train arrived at the station for Malory Towers at last. Out poured the girls, complete with night cases and rackets, and rushed to find good seats in the school coaches that took the train girls on the last part of their journey.

Felicity was tired and excited. Darrell didn't seem in the least tired, but she was certainly excited. "Now we shall see the school, and all the rest of the girls," she said to Felicity, happily. "Watch for the first glimpse of it when I tell you."

And so Felicity had the same first glimpse that Darrell had had four years back. She saw a large castle-like building of grey stone rising high on a hill. Beyond was the deep blue Cornish sea, but that was now hidden by the cliff on which Malory Towers stood. Four towers stood at the corners of the building, and Felicity's eyes brightened as she thought of sleeping in one of the towers. She would be in North Tower with Darrell – and it had the best view of the sea! She was very lucky.

"It's lovely," said Felicity to Darrell, and Darrell was pleased. It was going to be nice to have her sister at school with her. She felt sure that Felicity would be a great success.

Girls who had already arrived by car stood about the drive ready to welcome the train girls. There were shrieks and squeals of delight as the coaches drove up to the magnificent front entrance, and swarms of girls ran to help down their friends.

"Hallo, Belinda!" shouted Irene, climbing down and leaving behind her night case. "Done any decent sketching?"

"Darrell!" called a shy-looking fifteen-year-old. "Sally! Alicia!"

"Hallo, Mary-Lou! Anyone put a spider down your neck these hols?" cried Alicia. "Seen Betty?"

Betty was Alicia's friend, as witty as she was, and as mischievous. She came up and banged Alicia on the back.

"Here I am! You're jolly late – the train must have been even later than usual!"

"There's Mavis," cried Sally. "And Daphne – and I say, hallo there, Jean. Seen Bill anywhere?"

"Yes. She came on Thunder as usual and she's in the stable with him," said Jean, the quiet, shrewd Scots girl, who was now no longer in the same form as Darrell, but was going up. "She came with the groom, because all her brothers went back to school before we did this term. A very tame arrival!"

Felicity stood unheeded in the general rush and excitement. She hoped that Darrell would entirely forget her. Alicia had completely forgotten about her cousin June. That youngster now came up to Felicity and grinned. "Our elders are making a fine noise, aren't they?" she said. "We're small fry to them. Let's slip off by ourselves, shall we, and make them look for us when they deign to remember we're here?"

"Oh, no," said Felicity, but June pulled her arm and dragged her away. "Yes, come on. I know we're supposed to go to Matron and give in our health certificate and our term's pocket money. We'll go and find her on our own."

"But Darrell won't like . . ." began Felicity, as she was led firmly away by June.

So it was when Darrell looked round for her young sister, she was nowhere to be seen!

"Where's Felicity?" she said. "Blow! What's happened to her? I know how awful you feel when you're new, and I wanted to take her under my wing for a bit. Where in the world has she gone?"

"Don't worry," said Alicia, unfeelingly. "I'm not bothering about young June. She can look after herself all right, if I know anything about that young lady. She's got all the cheek in the world!"

"Well, but Felicity hasn't," said Darrell. "Dash it, where has she gone? She was here a minute ago."

"Anyone seen my night case?" came Irene's voice in a mournful wail.

Nobody had. "You must have left it on your coach seat," suggested Darrell, knowing Irene's scatter-brain ways. Irene darted off after the coaches, which were now making their way slowly down the drive. "Hie, hie!" she yelled. "Wait a bit!"

"What *is* Irene doing?" said Miss Potts, crossly. "Irene, come back and stop shouting."

But Irene had stopped a coach and was climbing up into the one she had ridden in to the school. Miss Potts gaped. Did Irene think she was going home again? She did such mad things that anything was likely with Irene.

But Irene found her night case, waved it wildly in the air to show the others she had found it, and climbed down again to the drive. She ran back grinning.

"Got it!" she said, and stood it firmly down on the ground – too firmly, because it at once burst open and everything fell out.

"Oh, *Irene* – why does every case you possess always do that?" said Darrell, helping her to pick everything up.

"I can't imagine," said Irene, stuffing everything in higgledy-piggledy. "I have a bad effect on them, I suppose. Come on, let's go and find Matron."

"I haven't found Felicity yet," said Darrell, beginning to look worried. "She can't have gone off with anyone because she doesn't *know* anyone."

"Well, anyhow, let's go to Matron and hand in our health certificates and money, and ask if she's seen Felicity," said Sally. "The drive's pretty well empty now – she's obviously not here."

So they trailed off to Matron, who had been dealing most efficiently with dozens of girls, health certificates and pocket money for an hour or more. Darrell was pleased to see her – kindly, bustling, starched and competent.

"Hallo, Darrell! Well, Alicia, turned up again like a bad penny, I see!"

"Mother says you always used to say that to *her* when she came back each term," said Alicia, with a grin.

"Yes. She was a bad lot," said Matron, smiling. "Not nearly as bad as you, though, Alicia. We'll have to have a talk about 'How to Darn' this term, by the way. Don't forget. Aha, Irene, there you are at last. Got your health certificate?"

14

It was a standing joke that Irene's health certificate always got lost if Irene was given it to bring to Matron. But the last few terms Irene's mother had sent the certificate by post, so it had always arrived safely on the morning of the day that school began.

Irene looked alarmed. Then she smiled. "You're pulling my leg, Matron," she said. "It's come by post as usual."

"But it hasn't," said Matron. "That's the whole point. Plenty of post for me this morning – but no health certificate. It's probably in your night case, Irene. Go and unpack it and look."

Darrell was looking round for Felicity, but still she couldn't see her. She really felt very worried and rather cross. Why hadn't Felicity done as she was told, and kept close by her, so that she couldn't lose her in the crowd of girls?

"Matron," she said, "you haven't by any chance seen my little sister, have you?"

"Yes," said Matron. "She was here a few minutes ago, and handed in her health certificate. She said you had her money. Nice to have her here, Darrell."

Darrell was astonished. Felicity had actually gone to Matron and given in her own certificate without waiting to be taken! It didn't seem like Felicity at all – she was so shy.

"Where's she gone now?" she wondered out loud.

"She's gone to have a look at her dormy," said Matron, and turned to deal with Belinda, who seemed to have lost all her money and was turning out her pockets in despair. "Belinda! I vow and declare that I'll ask Miss Grayling to put you and Irene into another Tower next term. If I have to deal with you two much more I shall go raving mad. Sally, go and see if Irene has found her health certificate yet."

Sally went off to find Irene in the dormy, and

Darrell went off to find Felicity. Sally found Irene sitting mournfully on her bed, the contents of her night case strewn on the eiderdown – but there was no health certificate there.

"Oh, Irene – you really are a mutt," said Sally, rummaging round and shaking out the legs of Irene's pyjamas just in case she had put the precious piece of paper there. "I thought your mother always posted the certificate now."

"She *does*," groaned Irene. "She never fails. She's marvellous like that."

"Well, all I can say is that she must have given it to *you* to post this time!" said Sally. "And you must have forgotten."

A sudden light spread over Irene's humorous face. She slapped Sally on the back. "Sally, you've got it!" she said. "That's just what happened! Mother *did* give it to me to post, and I forgot it."

"Well, where did you put it? Left it on your bedroom table at home, I suppose?" said Sally, half-impatient.

"No. I didn't," said Irene, triumphantly. "I put it into the lining of my hat, so that I shouldn't lose it on the way to the post – but when I got to the Post Office, I just bought some stamps and walked home again. So the certificate should be in my hat lining still. In fact, I'm sure it is because now I come to think of it, my hat felt jolly uncomfortable all day long."

It took some time to find Irene's hat, which had rolled under the next bed – but to Irene's joy the envelope with the certificate in was actually still under the lining. She shot off to Matron joyfully with it.

"I put it in my hat to remember to post it," she explained, "but I forgot, so it came with me today still in my hat."

16

Matron didn't understand a word of this, but dismissed it as all part of Irene's usual irresponsibility, and thankfully took the certificate before Irene could possibly lose it again.

"Did Darrell find her young sister?" she asked Irene.

But Irene didn't know. "I'll go and find out," she said, and wandered off again.

Darrell *had* found Felicity. She had found her in the dormy of the first-form, with June and several others. June was talking away to everyone as if she was a third-termer, and Felicity was standing by shyly, listening.

"Felicity!" said Darrell, going up to her. "Why didn't you wait for me? Whatever made you go to find Matron by yourself? You knew I was going!"

"Oh, *I* took her," said June. "I thought she might as well come with me. We're both new. I knew Alicia wouldn't bother herself with me and I didn't think you'd want to bother yourself with Felicity. We've given in our certificates but you've got to give in Felicity's money."

"I know that," said Darrell, very much on her dignity. What cheek of this new first-former to talk to her like that! She turned to Felicity.

"I do think you might have waited," she said. "I wanted to show you your dormy and everything."

The First Evening

Darrell went back to her own dormy to unpack her

night things, feeling puzzled and cross. She had so much looked forward to taking Felicity round and showing her her dormy, her bed and every single thing. How *could* her young sister have gone off with June and not waited for her?

"Did you find Felicity?" asked Alicia.

"Yes," said Darrell, shortly. "She'd gone off with that cousin of yours – what's her name – June. It struck me as rather extraordinary. You'd think these youngsters would wait for us to take them round a bit. I know I'd have been glad to have a sister or a cousin here, the first term *I* came."

"Oh, June can stand on her own feet very well," said Alicia. "She's a hard and determined little monkey. She'll always find things out for herself – and as for taking her under my wing, I wouldn't dream of putting anyone so prickly and uncomfortable there! Wait till you hear her argue! She can talk the hind leg off a donkey."

"I don't like the sound of her much," said Darrell, hoping that June wouldn't take Felicity under *her* wing. Surely Felicity wouldn't like anyone like June!

"No. She's a bit brazen," said Alicia. "We all are! Fault of my family, you know."

Darrell looked at Alicia. She didn't sound as if she minded it being a fault – in fact she spoke rather as if she were proud of it. Certainly Alicia was sharp-tongued and hard, though her years at Malory Towers had done a great deal to soften her. The trouble was that Alicia's brains and health were too good! She could always beat anyone else if she wanted to, without any effort at all – and Darrell didn't think she had ever had even a chilblain or a headache in her life. So she was always very scornful of illness or weakness in any form as well as contemptuous of stupidity.

Darrell determined to see as much of Felicity as

she could. She wasn't going to have her taken in tow by any brazen cousin of Alicia's. Felicity was young and shy, and more easily led than Darrell. Darrell felt quite fiercely protective towards her as she thought of the cheeky, determined young June.

They all unpacked their night cases and set out their things for the night. Their trunks, most of them sent on in advance, would not be unpacked till the next day. Darrell looked round her dormy, glad to be back.

It was a nice dormy, with a lovely view of the sea, which was as deep blue as a delphinium that evening. Far away the girls could hear the faint plash-plash of waves on the rocks. Darrell thought joyfully of the lovely swimming pool, and her heart lifted in delight at the thought of the summer term stretching before her – nicest term in the year!

The beds stood in a row along the dormy, each with its own coloured eiderdown. At the ends of the dormy were hot and cold water taps and basins.

Irene was splashing in one basin, removing the dust of the journey. She always arrived dirtier than anyone else. No one would ever guess that the scatterbrain was a perfect genius at music and maths, and quite good at her other lessons too! Everyone liked Irene, and everyone laughed at her.

She was humming a tune now as she washed. "Tumpty-tooty-tumpty-tooty, ta, ta, ta!"

"Oh, Irene – don't say we're going to have that tune for weeks," groaned Gwendoline, who always complained that Irene's continual humming and singing got on her nerves.

Irene took no notice at all, which maddened Gwendoline, who loved to be in the limelight if she possibly could.

"*Irene*," she began, but at that moment the door opened and in came two new girls, ushered by Matron.

19

"Girls – here are the Batten twins," she said in her genial voice. "Connie – and Ruth. They are fourth-formers and will be in this dormy. Look after them, Sally and Darrell, will you?"

The girls stood up to look at the twins. Their first thought was – how unlike for twins!

Connie was bigger, fatter, sturdier and bolder-looking than Ruth, who was a good deal smaller, and rather shy-looking. Connie smiling broadly and nodded to everyone. Ruth hardly raised her head to look round, and as soon as she could she stood a little way behind her sister.

"Hallo, twins!" said Alicia. "Welcome to the best dormy in the school! Those must be your beds up there – the two empty ones together."

"Got your night cases?" said Darrell. "Good. Well, if you'd like to unpack them now, you can. Supper will be ready soon. The bell will go any minute."

"Hope it's good," said Connie, with a comradely grin. "I'm frightfully hungry. It's ages since we had tea."

"Yes – we get a wizard supper the first evening," said Sally. "I can smell it now!"

Connie and Ruth put their noses in the air and sniffed hungrily.

"The Bisto twins!" said Alicia, hitting the nail right on the head as usual. Everyone laughed.

"Come on," said Connie to Ruth. "Let's hurry. I've got the keys. Here they are."

She undid both bags and dragged out everything quickly. Ruth picked up a few things and looked round rather helplessly.

"Here. These must be our drawers, next to our beds," said Connie, and began to put away all the things most efficiently. She took the washing things to the basin and called Ruth.

"Come on, Ruth. We'd better wash. I'm filthy!" Ruth went to join her, and just as they were towelling themselves dry, the supper bell went. There was a loud chorus of joy.

"Hurrah! I hope there's a smashing supper. I could do with roast duck, green peas, new potatoes, treacle pudding and lots of cheese," said Belinda, making everyone's mouth water.

"What a hope!" said Darrell.

But all the same there was a most delicious supper that first night – cold ham and tomatoes, great bowls of salad, potatoes roasted in their jackets, cold apple pie and cream, and biscuits and butter for those who wanted it. Big jugs of icy-cold lemonade stood along the table.

"My word!" said Connie to Ruth. "If this is the kind of food we get here, we'll be lucky! Much better than the other school we went to!"

"I hate to undeceive you," said Alicia, "but I feel I *must* warn you that first-night and last-night suppers are the *only* good ones you'll get in any term. We're supposed to be jolly hungry after our long journeys to Cornwall – hence this spread. Tomorrow night, twins, you'll have bread and dripping and cocoa."

As usual Alicia was exaggerating, and the twins looked rather alarmed. Darrell looked round for Felicity. Where was she? She couldn't have her at the Upper Fourth table, of course, but she hoped she would be near enough to say a word to.

She was too far away to speak to – and she was next to that nasty little June! June was talking to her animatedly, and Felicity was listening, enthralled.

Alicia saw Darrell looking across at Felicity and June. "They've soon settled in!" she said to Darrell. "Look at young Felicity listening to June. You should

21

hear the tales June can tell of her family! They're all madcaps, like mine."

Darrell remembered how interesting and amusing Alicia could be when she produced one of her endless yarns about her happy-go-lucky, mischievous family. She supposed that June was the same – but all the same she felt rather hurt that Felicity should apparently need her so little.

"Well, if she thinks she can get on by herself, all right!" thought Darrell. "I suppose it's best for her really – though I can't help feeling a bit disappointed. I suppose that horrid little June will find out everything she needs to know and show Felicity the swimming pool, the gardens, the stables, and all the things I'd planned to show her."

Felicity badly wanted to go to Darrell after supper and ask her a few things, but as soon as she said she was going, June pulled her back.

"You mustn't!" said June. "Don't you know how the older ones hate having young sisters and cousins tagging after them? Everyone will be bored with us if we go tailing after Alicia and Darrell. In fact, Alicia told me I'd jolly well better look after myself, because first-formers were such small fry we weren't even worth taking notice of!"

"How horrid of her," said Felicity. "Darrell's not like that."

"They all are, the big ones," said June in a grown-up voice. "And why *should* they be bothered with us? We've got to learn to stand on our own feet, haven't we? No – you wait till your sister comes over to you. If she doesn't, you'll know she doesn't want to be bothered – and if she does, well don't make her feel you're dependent on her and want taking under her wing. She'll respect you much more if you stand on your own feet. She looks as if she stood on her own all right!"

22

"She does," said Felicity. "Yes, perhaps you're right, June. I've often heard Darrell speak scornfully of people who can't stand on their own feet, or make up their own minds. After all – most new girls haven't got sisters to see to them. I suppose I shouldn't expect mine to nurse me, just because I've come to a new school."

June looked at her so approvingly that Felicity couldn't help feeling pleased. "I'm glad you're not a softy," said June "I was afraid you might be. Hallo – here comes Darrell after all. Now, don't weep on her shoulder."

"As if I should!" said Felicity, indignantly. She smiled at Darrell as she came over.

"Hallo, Felicity. Getting on all right?" said Darrell, kindly. "Want any help or advice with anything?"

"Thanks awfully, Darrell – but I'm getting on fine," said Felicity, wishing all the same that she might ask Darrell a few things.

"Like to come and see the swimming pool?" said Darrell. "We might just have time."

Darrell had forgotten that the first-formers had to go to bed almost immediately after supper on the first night. But June knew it. She answered for Felicity.

"We've got to go to bed, so Felicity won't be able to see it tonight," she said, coolly. "We planned to go down tomorrow before breakfast. The tide will be in then. I've asked."

"I was speaking to Felicity, not to you," said Darrell, in the haughty tones of a fourth-former. "Don't get too big for your boots, June, or you'll be sat on." She turned to Felicity and spoke rather coldly.

"Well, I'm glad you're settling down, Felicity. Sorry you're not in my dormy, but only fourth-formers are there, of course."

A bell rang loudly. "Our bedtime bell," said June, who appeared to know everything. "We'd better go. I'll look after Felicity for you, Darrell."

And with that the irrepressible June linked her arm in Felicity's and dragged her off. Darrell was boiling with rage. She gazed angrily after the two girls, and was only slightly mollified when Felicity turned round and gave her a sweet and rather apologetic smile.

"The brazen cheek of that little pest of a June!" thought Darrell. "I've never wanted to slap anyone so much in my life."

All Together Again

Going to bed on the first night was always fun, especially in the summer term, because then the windows were wide open, daylight was still bright, and the view was glorious.

It was lovely to be with so many girls again too, to discuss the holidays, and to wonder what the term would bring forth.

"School Cert. to be taken this term," groaned Daphne. "How simply horrible. I've been coached for it all the hols, but I don't feel I know much even now."

"Miss Williams will keep our noses to the grindstone this term," said Alicia, dolefully.

"Well, *you* don't need to mind," said Bill. She had spoken very little so far, and the others had left her alone. They knew she got, not homesick, but "horse-sick" as she called it, the first night or two back at school. She was passionately attached to all the horses owned by her parents and her seven brothers, and missed them terribly at first.

Alicia looked at her. "Why don't I need to mind?" she said. "I mind just as much as you do!"

"Well, I mean you don't really need to work, Alicia," said Bill. "You seem to learn things without bothering. I've been coached in the hols, too, and it was an awful nuisance just when I was wanting to ride with my brothers. I jolly well had to work, though. I bet *you* weren't coached in the hols."

"Mavis, are *you* going in for School Cert.?" asked Darrell. Mavis had been very ill the year before, and had lost her voice. It had been a magnificent voice, but her illness had ruined it. She had always said she was going to be an opera singer, but nobody ever heard her mention it now. In fact, most of the girls had even forgotten that Mavis had had a wonderful voice.

"I'm going in all right," said Mavis. "But I shan't get through! I feel like a jelly when I think of it. By the way – did you know my voice is getting right again?"

There was a pause whilst the girls remembered Mavis's lost voice. "Gosh! Is it really?" said Sally. "Good for you, Mavis! Fancy being able to sing again."

"I mayn't sing much," said Mavis. "But I shall know this term, I expect, if my voice will ever be worth training again."

"Good luck to you, Mavis," said Darrell. She remembered that when Mavis had had her wonderful voice they had all thought the girl was a Voice and nothing else at all – just a little nobody without an ounce of character. But now Mavis had plenty of character, and it was quite difficult to remember her Voice.

"I wonder if she'll go back to being a Voice and nothing else," thought Darrell. "No – I don't think she will. She deserves to get her voice back again. She's never complained about it, or pitied herself."

"I say!" said Mary-Lou's voice, "who's this bed for, at my end of the room? There are nobody's things here."

The girls counted themselves and then the beds. "Yes – that bed's over," said Darrell. "Well, it wouldn't have been put up if it hadn't been going to be used. There must be another new girl coming."

"We'll ask tomorrow," said Alicia, yawning. "How are you getting on, twins? All right?"

The two new girls answered politely. "Fine, thank you." They had washed, cleaned their teeth, brushed their hair, and were already in bed. Darrell had been amused to see that Connie had looked after Ruth as if she had been a younger sister, turning down her bed for her, and even brushing her hair!

She looked at them as they lay in bed, their faces turned sleepily towards her. Connie's face was plump and round, and her thick hair was quite straight. She had a bold look about her – "sort of pushful", thought Darrell. The other twin, Ruth, had a small heart-shaped face, and her hair, corn-coloured as Connie's, was wavy.

"Good night," said Darrell, and grinned. They grinned back. Darrell thought she was going to like them. She wished they had been absolutely alike though – that would have been fun! But they were really very unalike indeed.

One by one the girls got yawning into bed and snuggled down. Most of them threw their eiderdowns off, because the May night was warm. Gwendoline kept hers on. She always liked heaps of coverings, and nobody had ever persuaded her to go without her quilt in the summer.

Miss Potts looked in. Some of the girls were already

26

asleep. "No more talking," said Miss Potts, softly. A few grunts were made in reply. Nobody wanted to talk now.

Darrell wondered suddenly if Felicity was all right. She hoped she wasn't homesick. She wouldn't have time to be if June was in the next bed, talking away! What an unpleasant child! thought Darrell. And the cheek she had! It was past believing.

When the bell rang for getting up the next morning, there was a chorus of groans and moans. Nobody stirred out of bed.

"Well – we *must* get up!" said Darrell at last. "Come on, everybody! Gracious, look at Gwendoline – still fast asleep!"

Darrell winked at Sally. Gwendoline was not fast asleep, but she meant to have a few more minutes' snooze.

"She'll be late," said Sally. "Can't let her get into trouble her very first morning. Better squeeze a cold sponge over her, Darrell!"

This remark, made regularly about twenty times every term, always had the desired effect. Gwendoline opened her eyes indignantly, and sat up. "Don't you dare to squeeze that sponge over me," she began angrily. "This beastly getting up early! Why, at home . . ."

"Why, at home 'We don't get up till eight o'clock,' " chanted some of the girls, and laughed. They knew Gwendoline Mary's complaints by heart now.

"Did your old governess make her darling's bed for her?" asked Alicia. "Did she tie her bib on her in the morning? Did she feed her sweet Gwendoline Mary out of a silver spoon?"

Gwendoline had had to put up with Alicia's malicious teasing for many terms now, but she had never got used to it. The easy tears came to her eyes, and she turned her head away.

28

"Shut up, Alicia," said Darrell. "Don't start on her too soon!"

Alicia nudged Sally, and nodded towards the twins. Connie was making Ruth's bed for her!

"I can do that," protested Ruth, but Connie pushed her aside. "I've time, Ruth. You're slow at things like this. I always did it for you at our other school, and I can go on doing it here." She looked round at the others, and saw them watching her.

"Any objection?" she asked, rather belligerently.

"Dear me no," said Alicia in her smooth voice. "You can do mine for me, as well, if you like! I'm slow at things like that, too!"

Connie didn't think this remark was worth answering. She went on making Ruth's bed. Ruth was standing by, looking rather helpless.

"What school have you come from?" asked Darrell, speaking to Ruth. But before the girl could answer, Connie had replied.

"We went to Abbey School, in Yorkshire. It was nice – but not as nice as this one's going to be!"

That pleased the fourth-formers. "Did you play hockey or lacrosse at your other school?" asked Sally, addressing her question to Ruth.

"Hockey," said Connie, answering again, "I liked hockey – but I wanted to play lacrosse, too."

"Will *you* like lacrosse, do you think?" asked Sally, addressing her question once more to Ruth, wondering if she had a tongue.

And once again Connie answered: "Oh, Ruth always likes what *I* like! She'll love lacrosse!"

Sally was just about to ask if Ruth ever said a word for herself, when the breakfast bell rang. The girls hastily looked round the dormy to see if any clothes had been left about, and Alicia hurriedly pulled her quilt straight. Gwendoline was last as usual, moaning

29

about a lost hairgrip. But then Gwen always had a moan! Nobody took much notice of that!

Darrell looked anxiously for Felicity as the girls filed into the big dining-room, all the North Tower girls together. South Tower girls fed in the South Tower, East in the East and so on. Each tower was like a separate boarding-house, with its own common-rooms, dining-rooms and dormies. The class-rooms were in the long buildings that joined tower to tower, and so were such special rooms as the lab., the art-room and the sewing-room. The magnificent gym was there, too.

Felicity came in, looking neat and tidy. Miss Potts, seeing her come in, thought how very like she was to Darrell four years ago, when she also had come timidly into the dining-room for her first breakfast.

In front of Felicity was June, looking as if she was at least a third-termer, instead of a new girl on her first morning. She looked about chirpily, nodded at Alicia, who did her best not to see, grinned at Darrell, who stared stonily back, and spoke amiably to Mam'zelle Dupont, who was at the head of the first-form table. The second form were also there, and Darrell and Alicia had the satisfaction of seeing two second-formers push June roughly back when she attempted to sit somewhere near the head of the table.

But nothing daunted June. She merely sat down somewhere else, and said something to Felicity, who grinned uneasily. "Something cheeky, I bet," thought Darrell to herself. "Well, her form will put her in her place pretty soon – and she'll come up against the second form, too. There are some tough kids in the second – they won't stand much nonsense from a pest like June!"

Felicity smiled at Darrell, who smiled back warmly, forgetting for the moment that Felicity had probably

30

gone to see the swimming pool before breakfast without her. She hoped her little sister would do well in the class tests that day and prove that she was up to standard.

Sally suddenly remembered the empty bed in her dormy, and she spoke to Miss Potts.

"Miss Potts! There's an extra bed in our dormy. Do you know whose it is? We're all back."

"Oh, yes," said Miss Potts. "Let me see – there's one more new girl coming today – what's her name now – Clarissa something – yes, Clarissa Carter. That reminds me – there's a letter for her already. Here it is, Sally – put it up on her dressing table for her, will you?"

Gwendoline took the letter to pass it down the table. She glanced at it, and then looked again. The letter was addressed to "The Honourable Clarissa Carter".

"The *Honourable* Clarissa Carter!" thought Gwendoline, delighted. "If only she'd be my friend! I'll look after her when she comes. I'll do all I can!"

Gwendoline was a little snob, always hanging round those who were rich, beautiful or gifted. Alicia grinned as she saw the girl's face. "Gwendoline's going all out for the Honourable Clarissa," she thought. "Now we shall see some fun!"

An Interesting Morning

The Upper Fourth were taken by Miss Williams, a scholarly, prim mistress, whose gentleness did not mean any lack of discipline. As a rule the Upper

31

Fourth were a good lot, responsible and hard-working – but this year Miss Williams had sometimes had trouble with her form. There were such a lot of scatter-brains in it!

"Still I think they will all get through the School Cert.," thought Miss Williams. "They are none of them *really* stupid, except Gwendoline. Daphne is much better since she has had regular coaching in the holidays. Mavis has picked up wonderfully. So has Bill. And though little Mary-Lou is quite sure she will fail, she is quite certain to pass!"

Her form did not only consist of the North Tower girls, but of the fourth-formers from the other towers. Betty Hill, Alicia's friend, was one of these. She was as quick-tongued as Alicia, but not as quick-brained. She came from West Tower, and Alicia and she had often groaned because the authorities were so hard-hearted that they would not let Betty join Alicia in North Tower!

Miss Grayling, the Headmistress, had once asked Miss Potts, North Tower's house mistress, if she could change Betty Hill over to North Tower, as Betty's parents had actually written to ask if she would.

"I can manage Alicia alone," said Miss Potts, "or even Betty alone – but to have those two together in one house would be quite impossible. I should never have a moment's peace – and neither would Mam'zelle."

"I agree with you," said Miss Grayling. So a letter was sent to Mr and Mrs Hill regretting that it was impossible to find room for Betty in North Tower. Still, Alicia and Betty managed to be very firm friends indeed, although they were in different towers, meeting in class each day, arranging walks and expeditions together – and planning various wicked and amusing jokes and tricks.

32

The North Tower fourth-formers went eagerly to their classroom after Prayers. They wanted to choose their desks, and to sort out their things, to look out of the window, clean the blackboard, and do the hundred and one things they had done together so often before.

The twins stood and waited till the other girls had chosen their desks. They knew enough not to choose till then. By that time, of course, there were very few desks left – only those for two East Tower girls who were still not back, and for Clarissa Carter, and for themselves.

"We'll sit together, of course," said Connie, and put her books and Ruth's on two adjoining desks. They were, alas, in the hated front row, but naturally all the other rows had been taken, the back row going first. It was the only row really safe enough for whispering, or for passing a note or two.

Darrell looked out of the window, and wondered if Felicity had been to see Miss Grayling yet. She must ask her, when she saw her at Break. Miss Grayling saw all the new girls together, and what she said to them always impressed them, and made them determine to do their very best. Darrell remembered clearly how impressed she had been, and how she had made up her mind to be one of the worthwhile people of the world.

"I wonder who will be head girl this term," said Alicia, interrupting Darrell's thoughts. "Jean's gone up, so she won't be. Well – I bet *I* shan't be! I never have, and I don't expect I ever will. The Grayling doesn't trust me!"

"I expect Sally will be," said Darrell. "She was head of the second when we were in that form, and a jolly good head she made – though as far as I remember, you didn't approve at all, Alicia!"

"No, I didn't," said Alicia, candidly. "I thought *I*

ought to be head. But I've got rid of silly ideas like that now. I see that I'm not fitted to be head of anything – I just don't care enough."

Part of this was just bravado, but quite a bit of it was truth. Alicia *didn't* care enough! Things were so easy for her that she had never had to try hard for anything and so she didn't care. "If she had to work jolly hard at lessons, as I have to do," thought Darrell, "she'd care all right! We value the things we have to work hard for. Alicia does things too easily."

Gwendoline had chosen a seat in the front row! Everyone was most astonished, Alicia eyed her wonderingly. Could she be sucking up to Miss Williams? No, nobody in the world could do that. Miss Williams simply wouldn't notice it! Then what was the reason for Gwendoline's curious choice?

"Well, of *course*!" said Alicia, suddenly, and everyone gazed at her in surprise.

"Of course *what*?" said Betty.

"I've just thought why dear Gwendoline has chosen that front seat," said Alicia, maliciously. "At first I thought she'd gone out of her senses, but now I know!"

Gwendoline scowled at her. She was really afraid of Alicia's sly tongue, and she thought it quite likely that Alicia *had* hit on the correct reason.

But Alicia did not enlighten the class just then. She smiled sarcastically at Gwendoline and said, "Dear Gwen, I won't give you away – you really have a very *Honourable* reason for your choice, haven't you?"

Nobody could imagine what she meant, not even Betty – but Gwendoline knew! She had chosen a front desk because she knew that the Honourable Clarissa Carter would have to have one there, too – and it would be a very good thing to be next to her and help her!

She flushed red and said nothing, but busied herself

with her books. Miss Williams came in at that moment and Gwen rushed to hold the door.

The first day of school was always "nice and messy" as Belinda called it. No proper lessons were done, but tests were given out, principally to check up on the standard of any new girls. Timetables were made out with much groaning. Irene always gave hers up in despair. Although she was so good and neat at both maths and music, she was hopeless at a simple thing like making out her own timetable from the big class one.

It usually ended in Belinda doing it for her, but as Belinda wasn't much better, Irene was in a perpetual muddle over her timetable, appearing in the wrong classroom at the wrong time, expecting to have a maths lesson in the sewing room, or sewing lesson in the lab! All the mistresses had long ago given up expecting either Irene or Belinda to be sane and sensible in ordinary matters.

Irene, with her great gift for music, and Belinda, with her equally fine gift for drawing, seemed to become four-year-olds when they had to tackle ordinary everyday things. It was nothing for Irene to appear at breakfast time without her stockings, or for Belinda to lose, most inexplicably, every school book she possessed. The girls loved them for their amusing ways, and admired them for their gifts.

Everyone was busy with something or other that first morning. Darrell made out a list of classroom duties – filling up the ink-pots, doing the classroom flowers, keeping the blackboard clean, giving out necessary stationery and so on. Each of the class had to take on a week's duty, together with another girl, during the term.

Just before Break Miss Williams told the girls to tidy up their desks. "I have something to say to you," she said. "It will only take about two minutes, but it is something that I am sure you all want to know!"

"She's going to say who's to be head girl this term!" whispered Sally to Darrell. "Look at Gwendoline! See the look she's put on her face. She really thinks *she* might be!"

It was true. Gwendoline always hoped she might be head of the form, and had enough conceit to think she would make a very good one. Just as regularly she was disappointed, and always would be. Spoilt, selfish girls make poor heads, and no teacher in her senses would ever choose Gwendoline Mary!

"I think probably most of you will know that Jean, who passed School Cert. last year, has gone up into the next form," said Miss Williams. "She does not need to work with the School Cert. form this term. She was head girl of the Upper Fourth, and now that she has gone, we must have another."

She paused, and looked round the listening class. "I have discussed the matter with Miss Grayling, Miss Potts, Mam'zelles Dupont and Rougier," said Miss Williams. "We are all agreed that we would like to try Darrell Rivers as head girl."

Darrell flushed bright red and her heart beat fast. Everyone clapped and cheered, even Gwendoline, who always dreaded that Alicia might conceivably be chosen one day!

"I am quite sure, Darrell, that our choice is right," said Miss Williams, smiling her gentle smile at the blushing Darrell. "I cannot think for one moment that you would do anything to make us regret our choice."

"No, Miss Williams, I won't," said Darrell, fervently. She wished she could go and tell her parents this very minute. Head girl of the Upper Fourth! She had always wanted to be head of something, and this

36

was the first time her chance had come. She would be the very best head girl the form had ever had.

What would Felicity say? It would be a grand thing for Felicity to be able to say "my sister, of course, is head of the Upper Fourth!" Felicity would be proud and pleased.

Darrell rushed off at Break to find Felicity and tell her. But again she had disappeared. How absolutely *maddening*! Darrell only had a few minutes. She rushed round and about and at last found Felicity in the courtyard, with June. The courtyard was the space that lay inside the hollow oblong of the building that made up Malory Towers. It was very sheltered, and here everything was very early indeed. It was now bright with tulips, rhododendrons and lupins, and very lovely to see.

But Darrell didn't see the flowers that morning. She rushed at Felicity.

"Felicity! I've got good news for you – I've been made head girl of the Upper Fourth!"

"Oh, Darrell! How super!" said Felicity. "I'm *awfully* glad. Oh, Darrell, I must tell you – I saw Miss Grayling this morning, and she said to me, and all the other new girls, exactly the same things that she said to you, when *you* first came. She was grand!"

Darrell's mind took her back to her own first morning standing opposite Miss Grayling in her pleasant drawing room, hearing her talk gravely to the listening girls. She heard the Headmistress's voice.

"One day you will leave school, and go out into the world as young women. You should take with you a good understanding of many things, and a willingness to accept responsibility and show yourselves as women to be loved and trusted. I do not count as successes those who have won scholarships and passed exams, though these are good things to do. I count as our successes those who learn to be goodhearted and kind, sensible and trustable, good sound women the world can lean on."

Yes, Darrell remembered those long-ago words, and was very very glad she was beginning to be one of the successes – for had she not been chosen as head girl that very day, head of the Upper Fourth, the School Cert. form!

"Yes, Miss Grayling's grand," she said to Felicity.

"And *you're* grand, too!" said Felicity, proudly to Darrell. "It's *lovely* to have a head girl for a sister!"

Clarissa Arrives

Gwendoline was keeping a good look-out for the coming of the last new Upper Fourth girl, Clarissa. She was about the only girl in the form who had no special friend, and she could see that it wouldn't be much good trying to make friends with the twins, because they would only want each other.

"Anyway I don't like the look of them much," thought Gwendoline. "They'll probably go all out for games and gym and walks. Why aren't there any nice *feminine* girls here – ones who like to talk and read quietly, and not always go pounding about the lacrosse field or splash in that horrible pool!"

Poor lazy Gwendoline! She didn't enjoy any of the things that gave the others such fun and pleasure. She hated anything that made her run about, and she detested the cold water of the pool.

Daphne and Mary-Lou didn't like the pool either,

but they enjoyed tennis and walks. Neither of them went riding because they were terrified of horses. Bill, who now rode every day on Thunder before breakfast, scorned Daphne, Mary-Lou and Gwendoline because they wouldn't even offer Thunder a lump of sugar and screamed if he so much as stamped on the ground. She and Darrell and the new twins arranged an evening ride twice a week together, and Miss Peters, the third-form mistress, and Bill's great friend, came with them. They all enjoyed those rides on the cliffs immensely.

Felicity was not allowed to go with them because she was only a first-former. To Darrell's annoyance she learnt that the only other good rider in the first form was June, so once again it seemed as if Felicity and June were to be companions and enjoy something together.

"It'll end in Felicity having to make June her friend," thought Darrell. "Oh, dear – it's an awful pity I don't like June. Felicity likes Sally so much. We ought to like each other's friends. The mere *thought* of having June to stay with us in any holidays makes me squirm!"

The North Tower Upper Fourth girls paired off very well – except for Gwendoline. Sally always went with Darrell, of course. Irene and Belinda, the two clever madcaps, were inseparable, and very bad for each other. Alicia was the only one who had a friend from another Tower, and she and Betty were staunch friends.

Daphne and Mary-Lou were friends, and Mavis hung on to them when she could. They liked her and did not mind being a threesome sometimes. Bill had no special friend, but she didn't want one. Thunder was hers. Bill was better with boys than with girls, because having seven brothers she understood boys and not girls. She might have been a boy herself in

39

the way she acted. She was the only fourth-former who chose to learn carpentry from Mr Sutton, and did not in the least mind going with the first- and second-formers who enjoyed his teaching so much. She had already produced a pipe for her father, a ship for her youngest brother, and a bowl-stand for her mother, and was as proud of these as any of the good embroiderers were of their cushions, or the weavers of their scarves.

So it was really only Gwendoline who had no one to go with, no one to ask her for her company on a walk, no one to giggle with in a corner. She pretended not to mind, but she did mind, very much. But perhaps now she would have her chance when the Honourable Clarissa came. How pleased her mother would be if she had a really nice friend!

Gwendoline ran her mind back over the friends she had tried to make. There was Mary-Lou – stupid little Mary-Lou! There was Daphne, who had seemed to be so very friendly one term, and then had suddenly become friends with Mary-Lou! There was Mavis, who had had such a wonderful voice and was going to be an opera singer. Gwendoline would have liked such a grand person for a friend in after life.

But Mavis had fallen ill and lost her voice, and Gwendoline didn't want her any more. Then there had been Zerelda, the American girl who had now left – but she had no time for Gwendoline!

Gwendoline thought mournfully of all these failures. She didn't for one moment think that her lack of friends was her own fault. It was just the horridness of the other girls! If only, only, only she could find somebody like herself – somebody who had never been to school before coming to Malory Towers, who had only had a governess, who didn't play games and somebody who had wealthy parents who would ask her to go and stay in the holidays!

So Gwendoline waited in hopes for Clarissa's arrival. She imagined a beautiful girl with lovely clothes, arriving in a magnificent car – the Honourable Clarissa! "*My* friend," thought Gwendoline, and she imagined herself at half term saying to her mother and Miss Winter, her old governess, "Mother, I want you to meet the Honourable Clarissa Carter, my best friend!"

She did not tell any of the girls these thoughts. She knew the words they would use to her if they guessed what she was planning – snob, hypocrite, fraud! Sucking up to somebody! Just like dear Gwendoline Mary!

Clarissa did not arrive till tea time. Gwendoline was sitting at table with the others, so she did not see her until the Headmistress suddenly appeared with a strange girl.

Gwendoline looked up without much interest. The girl was small and undersized-looking – a second-former perhaps. She wore glasses with thick lenses, and had a wire round her teeth to keep them back. Her only beauty seemed to be her hair, which was thick and wavy, and a lovely auburn colour. Gwendoline took another slice of bread and butter and looked for the jam.

The new girl was so nervous that she was actually trembling! Darrell noticed that and was sorry for her. She too had felt like trembling when she first came, and had faced so many girls she didn't know – and here was a poor creature who really *was* trembling!

To Darrell's surprise Miss Grayling brought the girl up to the Upper Fourth table. Mam'zelle Dupont was taking tea and sat at the head.

"Oh, Mam'zelle," said Miss Grayling, "here is Clarissa Carter, the last new girl for the Upper Fourth. Can you find a seat for her and give her some tea? Then perhaps your head girl can look after her when tea is finished."

Gwendoline almost dropped her bread and butter in surprise. Goodness, she had nearly missed her chance! Could this small, ugly girl really be Clarissa? It was, so she must hurry up and put her plan into action.

There was a space beside Gwendoline and she stood up in such a hurry that she almost knocked over Daphne's cup of tea. "Clarissa can sit by me," she said. "There is room here."

Clarissa, only too glad to sit down and hide herself, sank gladly into the place beside Gwendoline. Alicia nudged Darrell. "Got going quickly, hasn't she?" she whispered, and Darrell chuckled.

Gwendoline was at her very sweetest. "Sickly-sweet" was the name given by Alicia to this particular form of friendliness shown by Gwendoline. She leant towards Clarissa and smiled in a most friendly way.

"Welcome to Malory Towers! I expect you are tired and hungry. Have some bread and butter."

"I don't think I could eat any, thank you," said Clarissa, almost sick with nervousness. "Thank you all the same."

"Oh, you must have *some*thing!" said Gwendoline and took a piece of bread and butter. "I'll put some jam on it for you. It's apricot – very nice for a change."

Clarissa didn't dare to object. She sat huddled up as if she wanted to make herself as small and unnoticeable as possible. She nibbled at the bread and butter, but couldn't seem to eat more than a bit of it.

Gwendoline chattered away, thinking how good and sweet she must seem to the others, putting this nervous new girl at her ease in such a friendly manner. But only Mam'zelle was deceived.

"The dear kind Gwendoline," she thought. "Ah, she is a stupid child at her French, but see how charming

42

she is to this poor plain girl, who shakes with nerves."

"Sucking up," said everyone else round the table. They said nothing to Clarissa, feeling that it was enough for the new girl to cope with Gwen, without having to deal with anyone else as well. Mary-Lou liked the look of Clarissa, in spite of her thick glasses and wire round her front teeth – but then Mary-Lou always felt friendly towards anyone as timid as herself! They were about the only people she wasn't afraid of.

After tea Mam'zelle spoke to Darrell. "Darrell, you will take care of Clarissa, *n'est-ce pas*? She will feel strange at first, *la pauvre petite*!"

"Mam'zelle, I'm awfully sorry, but I've got to go to a meeting of all the head girls of the forms," said Darrell. "It's in five minutes' time. Perhaps Sally – or Belinda – or . . ."

"*I'll* look after her," said Gwendoline, promptly, thrilled that Darrell had to go to a meeting. "I'll show her round. I'll be very pleased to."

She gave Clarissa a beaming smile that startled the new girl and made everyone else feel slightly sick. She slipped her arm through Clarissa's. "Come along," she said, in a sort of voice one uses to a very small child. "Where's your night case? I'll show you the dormy. You've got a very nice place in it."

She went off with Clarissa, and everyone made faces and grinned. "Trust our Gwendoline Mary to show a bit of determination over things like this," said Alicia. "What a nasty little snob! Honestly, I don't think Gwendoline has altered one bit for the better since she came to Malory Towers!"

"I think you're right," said Darrell, considering the matter with her head on one side. "It's really rather strange – I would have thought that being even a few terms here would have made everyone better in some way – and Gwen has been here years – but she's just the same sly, mean, lazy little sucker-up!"

"How has it made *you* better, Darrell?" said Alicia, teasingly. "I can't say I've noticed much difference in *you*!"

"She was decent to start with," said Sally, loyally.

"Anyway, I've conquered my hot temper," said Darrell. "I haven't flown out in a rage for terms and terms – you know I haven't. That's one thing Malory Towers has done for me."

"Don't boast too soon," said Alicia, grinning. "I've seen a glint in your eye lately, Darrell – aha, yes I have! You be careful."

Darrell was about to deny this stoutly, when she stopped herself, and felt her cheeks going red. Yes – she *had* felt her eyes "glinting", as Alicia used to call it, when she spoke to that pest of a June. Well, she could "glint" surely, couldn't she? There was nothing wrong in that – so long as she didn't lose her temper, and she certainly wasn't going to do *that*!

"I'll 'glint' at you in a minute, Alicia," she said, with a laugh. "A head-girl 'glint' too – so just you be careful what you say!"

Darrell has a "Glint"

The Upper Fourth soon began to settle down to its work. Miss Williams was a fine teacher, and was quite determined to have excellent results in the School Certificate exam. Mam'zelle Dupont and Mam'zelle Rougier both taught the Upper Fourth, but though actually Mam'zelle Rougier was the better teacher, plump little Mam'zelle Dupont got better results because she was friendly and had a great sense of humour. The girls worked better for her than for the other Mam'zelle.

This term there was an armed truce between the two French mistresses. The English mistresses regarded them with great amusement, never knowing from one term to the next whether the two Frenchwomen would be bosom friends, bitter enemies, or dignified rivals.

Miss Carton, the history mistress, knew that the School Certificate form was well up to standard except for miseries like Gwendoline, who didn't even know the Kings of England and couldn't see that they mattered anyhow. She used her sarcastic tongue on Gwendoline a good deal these days, to try and whip her into some show of work, and Gwen hated her.

The girls grumbled because they had to work so hard in that lovely summer term. "Just when we want to go swimming, and play tennis, and laze about in the flowery courtyard, we've got to stew at our books," said Alicia. "I shall take my prep out into the open air tonight. I bet Miss Williams would let us."

Surprisingly Miss Williams said yes. She knew that she could trust most of the Upper Fourth not to play about when they were supposed to be working, and she thought that Darrell was a strong enough head girl to keep everyone up to the mark if necessary. So out they went after tea, and took cushions to sit on, in the evening sun.

Gwendoline didn't want to go. She was the only one, of course. "You really seem to *loathe* the open air," said Darrell, in surprise. "Come on out – a bit more fresh air and exercise would take off some of your fat and get rid of those spots on your nose."

"Don't make personal remarks," said Gwendoline, nose in air. "You're as bad as Alicia – and everyone

45

knows she's been dragged up, not brought up!"

Clarissa, who was with her, looked at Gwendoline in surprise. Gwen had been so sweet and gracious to her that it was quite a shock to hear her make a remark like this. Gwen was quick to see the look, and slipped her arm through Clarissa's.

"If *you're* taking your prep out, I'll take mine, of course," she said. "But let's sit away from the sun. I hate getting freckled."

Betty saw Alicia sitting out in the courtyard and came to join her. Darrell frowned. Now there would be nonsense and giggling and no work done. Belinda and Irene began to listen to the joke that Betty was telling Alicia, and Irene gave one of her sudden explosive snorts when it was finished. Everyone looked up, startled.

"Oh, I say, that's super!" roared Irene. "Here, Betty, tell the others."

Darrell looked up. She was head girl of the form, and she must stop this, she knew. She spoke out at once.

"Betty, stop gassing. Alicia, you know jolly well we're supposed to be doing our prep."

"Don't talk to me as if I was a first-former," said Alicia, nettled at Darrell's sharp tone.

"Well, I shall, if you behave like one," said Darrell.

"She's glinting, Alicia – look out, she's glinting!" said Irene, with a giggle. Everyone looked at Darrell and smiled. Darrell certainly had a "glint" in her eye.

"I'm not glinting," she said. "Don't be idiotic."

"I glint, though glintest, he glints, *she* glints!" chanted Betty. "We glint, you glint, they glint!"

"Shut up, Betty, and go away," said Darrell, feeling angry. "You don't belong to our prep. Go and join your own."

46

"I've done it, Miss Glint," said Betty. "Shall I help you with yours?"

To Darrell's horror, she felt the old familiar surge of anger creeping over her. She clenched her fists and spoke sharply to Betty again.

"You heard what I said. Clear out, or I'll take the whole of this prep back indoors."

Betty looked angry, but Alicia nudged her. "Go on. She's on the boil already. I'll meet you after we've done prep."

Betty went, whistling. Darrell bent her red face over her book. Had she been too dictatorial? But what were you to do with someone like Betty?

Nobody said anything more, and prep went peacefully on, accompanied by one or two groans from Irene and deep sighs from Gwendoline. Clarissa sat beside her, working slowly. Gwen copied whatever she could. Nobody could cure her of this habit, it seemed!

After an hour Miss Williams came into the courtyard, pleased to see the North Tower Upper Fourth working so peacefully and well.

"Time's up," she said. "And I've a message from your games mistress. The pool is just right now for bathing, so you can all go down there for half an hour, as you had to miss your bathe yesterday."

"Hurrah!" said Irene, and threw her book into the air. It went into the nearby pool, and had to be retrieved very hurriedly. "Idiot!" said Belinda, almost falling in herself as she tried to fish out the book. "I suppose you think that's *your* history book you're drowning. Well, it isn't – it's mine."

"Have we all *got* to go?" Gwendoline asked Miss Williams, pathetically. "I've been working so hard. I don't feel like swimming."

"Dear me – can you actually *swim* yet, Gwendoline?" said Miss Williams, with an air of surprise.

Everyone knew that Gwendoline could still only flap a few strokes in the water and then go under with a scream.

"Oh, we don't *all* need to go, do we?" said Mary-Lou, who could swim, but still didn't like the water much. Neither did Daphne, and she added her pleas to the others.

"You're all going," said Miss Williams. "You are having to work very hard, and these little relaxations are good for you. Go and change at once."

Thrilled at the thought of an unexpected evening bathe, Darrell, Sally and Alicia rushed to the changing room. Darrell had forgotten her annoyance with Alicia, but Alicia hadn't. Alicia bore malice, which was a pity. So she was rather cool to Darrell, who, most unfortunately for Alicia, didn't notice the coolness at all. The others followed, chattering and laughing, with a rather mournful tail composed of Gwen, Daphne and Mary-Lou. Clarissa came to watch. She was not allowed to swim or to play tennis because she had a weak heart.

"Lucky thing!" said Gwendoline, getting into her bathing suit. "No swimming, no tennis – I wish *I* had a weak heart."

"What a wicked thing to say," said Darrell, really shocked. "To wish yourself a thing like that! It must be simply horrible to keep on and on having to take care of yourself, and think, 'I mustn't do this, I mustn't do that'."

"It *is* horrible," said Clarissa, in her small shy voice. "If it hadn't been for my heart I'd not have been taught at home – I'd have come to school like any other girl. It's got much better lately though, and that's why I was allowed to come at *last*."

This was a long speech for Clarissa to make. Usually she was quite tongue-tied. As it was, she went red as

she spoke, and when she had finished she hung her head and tried to get behind Gwendoline.

"Poor old Clarissa," said Gwendoline, sympathetically. "You mustn't do too much, you know. Would you know if you *had* done too much?"

"Oh, yes. My heart begins to flutter inside me – as if I had a bird there or something," said Clarissa. "It's awful. It makes me want to lie down and pant."

"Really?" said Gwendoline, pulling her towel-wrap round her. "Well, you know, Clarissa, I shouldn't be a bit surprised if *I* hadn't a weak heart, too, that nobody knows about. If I try to swim for long I get absolutely panicky – and after a hot game of tennis my heart pumps like a piston. It's really painful."

"Nice to hear you *have* a heart," said Alicia, in her smoothest voice. "Where do you keep it?"

Gwendoline tossed her head and went off with Clarissa. "Beast, isn't she?" her voice floated back to the others. "I can't bear her. Nobody likes her really."

Alicia chuckled. "I'd love to know what sort of poisonous nonsense Gwendoline Mary is pouring into poor Clarissa's ears," she said. "I don't think we ought to let Gwendoline take complete charge of her like this. It's not fair. You ought to do something about it, Darrell. Why don't you?"

Darrell did not like this direct attack. She suddenly realized that Alicia was right – she ought to have made certain that Gwen didn't take such utter and complete charge of the rather weak little Clarissa. She would get all the wrong ideas in her very first term – and the ideas you had at the beginning were apt to stick!

"All right," she said, in a rather snappy tone. "Give me a chance! Clarissa has only been here a few days."

"My dear Darrell, you're glinting again," said

Alicia, with a laugh that provoked Darrell even more. She took hold of herself hastily. Really, she was getting quite touchy!

It was fun down at the pool. The good swimmers had races, of course. Mary-Lou bobbed up and down in the shallow end, swimming a few strokes every now and again. She always got in quickly, even though she hated the water. Daphne was in, too, shivering as usual, but bobbing beside Mary-Lou, hoping that Darrell wouldn't make her join in the racing. Mavis was swimming slowly. She had got over her dislike of the water, but had to be careful not to over-swim, or play too much tennis because of her illness the year before.

Only Gwendoline still stood shivering on the brink. Alicia, Sally and Darrell longed to push her in, but it was too much fag to get out of the pool.

"If Gwen doesn't get in soon, she won't get in at all," said Alicia. "Order her in, Darrell! Go on, put that glint in your eye, and give one of your orders!"

But not even Darrell's shouts persuaded poor Gwendoline to do more than wet her toes. She had got hot sitting in the courtyard and now the pool felt icy cold. Ooooh!

It was Clarissa who made her get in. She came running up to stand beside Gwendoline, slid on a slimy patch of rock, bumped hard into Gwendoline, and knocked her straight into the water!

Splash! In went Gwendoline with a terrible yell of fright. The girls clutched at one another and laughed till they cried. "Look at poor Clarissa's face," wept Darrell. "She's simply horrified!"

"Who did that?" demanded a furiously angry Gwendoline, bobbing up, and spitting out water. "Beasts, all of you!"

You're Head Girl, aren't you?

When Gwendoline heard that it was Clarissa who had pushed her in, she didn't believe it. She made her way over to where an apologetic Clarissa was standing.

"Who pushed me in, Clarissa?" she demanded. "They keep saying it was *you*, the idiots! As if you'd do a thing like that!"

"Oh, Gwendoline. I'm so very sorry but actually it *was* me," said Clarissa, quite distressed. "I slipped and fell, and bumped against you – and in you went. Of *course* I wouldn't have done it on purpose! I'm most terribly sorry about it!"

"Oh, that's all right then," said Gwendoline, pleased to see such a very apologetic Clarissa. "It did give me an awful shock, of course – and I hurt my foot against the bottom of the pool – but still, it was an accident."

Clarissa was more apologetic still, which was balm to Gwendoline's wounded feelings. She liked to have the Honourable Clarissa apologizing so humbly. She made up her mind to be very sweet and forgiving, and then Clarissa would think more than ever what a nice friend she was for anyone to have.

But the others spoilt it. They would keep coming up and yelling "Jolly good push!" to Clarissa, and "Well done, Clarissa – you got her in nicely!" and "I say, Clarissa, that was a fine shove. Do it again!"

"But I *didn't* push her," protested Clarissa, time and time again. "You know I didn't."

"Never seen such a good shove in my life!" said Alicia, and really, Gwendoline began to be quite doubtful as to whether Clarissa really *had* meant to push her or not! Then unfortunately Clarissa suddenly saw the funny side of all the shouted remarks and began to laugh helplessly. This made Gwen really cross, and she was so huffy with Clarissa that in great alarm Clarissa began to apologize all over again.

"Look at the twins," said Alicia to Sally. Sally looked and laughed. Connie was carefully rubbing Ruth dry, and Ruth was standing patiently, waiting for her sister to finish.

"Why doesn't Connie leave her alone?" said Sally. "Ruth can do everything for herself – but Connie always makes out she can't. She's too domineering for words!"

"And she's not nearly so good as Ruth is at lessons," said Alicia. "Ruth helps her every night, or she would never do the work. She's far behind Ruth."

"And yet she domineers over her the whole time!" said Darrell, joining in. "I hate to see it – and I hate to see Ruth putting up with it, too."

"Speak to her about it," said Alicia at once. "Head girl, aren't you?"

Darrell bit her lip. Why did Alicia keep on and on twitting her like this? She thought that perhaps it was partly envy – Alicia knew she would not really make a good head girl herself, and envied those who were, and tried to make them uncomfortable. She, Darrell, ought not to take any notice, but she couldn't help feeling annoyed about it.

"You've got a lot on hand now, haven't you," went on Alicia, rubbing herself dry. "Looking after young Felicity – seeing that Clarissa doesn't get too much poison from dear Gwendoline, trying to buck up Ruth a bit, and make her stand up for herself – ticking off Betty when she spoils our prep."

Darrell felt herself beginning to boil again. Then

a cool hand was laid on her shoulder, and she heard Sally's calm voice. "Everything in good time! It's a pity to rush things and spoil them – isn't it, Darrell? You can't put things right all at once."

Darrell heaved a sigh of relief. That was what *she* ought to have said – in a nice calm voice! Thank goodness Sally had said it for her!

She gave Sally a grateful smile. She determined to look up Felicity a bit more, and try to prise her away from that objectionable June. She would put one of the others on to Clarissa to offset Gwendoline's influence – and she would certainly have a few quiet words with Ruth, and tell her not to let Connie make such a baby of her.

"Why," thought Darrell, "it's quite absurd – whenever any of us speaks to Ruth, Connie always answers for her. I really wonder she doesn't answer for her in class, too!"

It was quite true that Ruth hardly ever answered for herself. Alicia might say to her, "Ruth, can you lend me that French dicky for a moment," but it would be Connie who said, "Yes, here's the dictionary – catch!"

And Sally might say, "Ruth, don't you want a new ruler – yours is broken," but it would be Connie who answered, "No, thanks, Sally, she can use mine."

It was annoying, too, to see how Connie always walked a little in front of Ruth, always offered an explanation of anything before her twin could say a word, always did any asking necessary. Hadn't Ruth got a soul of her own – or was she just a weak echo or shadow of her stronger twin?

It was a puzzle. Darrell decided to speak to Ruth the next day, and she found a good chance when both of them were washing painting jars in the cloakroom.

"How do you like Malory Towers, Ruth?" she

asked, wondering if Ruth would be able to answer, if Connie wasn't there!

"I like it," said Ruth.

"I hope you're happy here," said Darrell, wondering how to lead up to what she really wanted to say. There was a pause. Then Ruth answered politely.

"Yes, thank you."

She didn't sound happy at all, Darrell thought! Why ever not? She was well up to the standard of work, she was good at all games, there was nothing dislikeable about her – and the summer term was fun! She ought to be very happy indeed!

"Er – Ruth," said Darrell, thinking desperately that Sally would be much better at this kind of thing than she was, "– er – we think that you let yourself be – er – well, *nursed* a bit too much by Connie. Couldn't you – er – well, stand on your own feet a bit more? I mean . . ."

"I know what you mean all right," said Ruth, in a funny fierce voice. "If anyone knows what you mean, *I* do!"

Darrell thought that Ruth was hurt and angry. She tried again. "Of course I know you're twins – and twins are always so close to one another, and – and attached – so I quite understand Connie being so fond of you, and . . ."

"You don't understand anything at all," said Ruth. "Talk to Connie if you like, but you won't alter things one tiny bit!"

And with that she walked out stiffly, carrying her pile of clean paint jars. Darrell was left by herself in the cloakroom puzzled and rather cross.

"It's not going to be any good to talk to Connie, I'm sure," thought Darrell, rinsing out the last of the jars. "She'd be as fierce as Ruth. She's ruining Ruth! But if Ruth *wants* to be ruined, and made just a meek

55

shadow of Connie, well, let her! I can't see that I can stop her!"

She took her pile of paint jars away, and made up her mind that that particular difficulty could not be put right. "You can't drag twins away from each other if they've always been together and feel like one person," she decided. "Why, some twins know when the other is in pain or ill, even if they are far apart. It's no good putting those two against me. They must do as they like!"

The next thing to do was to ferret out Felicity, and see how she was getting on. She ought to be more or less settled down now. Perhaps she had made some more friends. If only she had others as well as June, it wouldn't matter so much – but Darrell felt that the strong-minded June would cling like a leech to someone like Felicity, if Felicity had no other friend at all!

So she found Felicity in Break, and asked her to come for a walk with her that evening. Felicity looked pleased. To go for a walk with the head girl of the Upper Fourth was a great honour.

"Oh, yes – I'd love to come," she said. "I don't think June's fixed anything for tonight."

"What does it matter if she has?" said Darrell, impatiently. "You can put her off, surely? I haven't seen anything of you lately."

"I like Miss Potts," said Felicity, changing the subject as she often did when Darrell got impatient. "I'm still a bit scared of her – but my work's a bit in advance of the form, really, Darrell, so I can sit back and take things easy this first term! Rather nice!"

"Yes, jolly nice," agreed Darrell. "That's what comes of going to a good prep school – you always find you're in advance of the lowest form work when you go to a public school – but if you go to a rotten prep school, it takes years to catch up! Er – how is

56

June in her work?"

"Brilliant — when she likes!" said Felicity, with a grin. "She's awfully good fun — frightfully funny, you know. Rather like Alicia, I should think."

"*Too* like Alicia," Darrell thought to herself, remembering how wonderful she had thought Alicia in *her* first term at Malory Towers. "Isn't there anyone else you like, Felicity?" she asked her sister.

"Oh, yes — I like most of my form," said Felicity. "They don't seem to like June much, though, and sit on her hard. But she's like indiarubber, bounces up again. There's one girl I like awfully — her name's Susan. She's been here two terms."

"Susan! Yes, she's fine," said Darrell. "Plays lacrosse awfully well for a kid — and she's good at gym, too. I remember seeing her in a gym display last term."

"Yes. She's good at games," agreed Felicity. "But June says Susan's too pi for words — won't do anything she shouldn't, and she thinks she's dull, too."

"She would!" said Darrell. "Well, I'm glad you like Susan. Why don't you make a threesome — you and June and Susan? I don't think June's a good person to have for an only friend."

"Why, you don't even know her!" said Felicity in surprise. "Anyway, *she* wouldn't want Susan in a threesome!"

A bell rang in the distance. "Well, see you this evening," said Darrell. "We'll go on the cliffs — but don't you go and bring June, mind! I want you to myself!"

"Right," said Felicity, looking pleased.

But alas, that evening a meeting was called of all the School Certificate girls, and Darrell had to go to it. She wondered if she could possibly squeeze time in for even a short walk with Felicity. No, she couldn't —

she had that essay to do as well.

She sent a message to her sister by a second-former. "Hey, Felicity," said the second-former, "compliments from Head Girl Darrell Rivers, and she says she can't take baby sister for a walky-walk tonight!"

Felicity stared at her indignantly. "You know jolly well she didn't say that!" she said. "What *did* she say?"

"Just that," said the cheeky second-former, and strolled off.

Felicity translated the message correctly and was disappointed.

"Darrell can't go for a walk tonight," she told June. "I suppose she's got a meeting or something."

"I bet she hasn't," said that young lady, scornfully. "I tell you, these fourth-formers, like Alicia and Darrell, don't *want* to be bothered with us – and we jolly well won't go bothering them! Come on – we'll go for a walk together!"

Gwendoline and Clarissa

Darrell forgot about Clarissa for a day or two, because for some reason the days suddenly became very full up indeed. Head girls seemed to have quite a lot of duties Darrell hadn't thought of, and there was such a lot of prep to do this term.

Gwendoline now had Clarissa very firmly attached to her side. She sat next to her in class, and offered to help her whenever she could – but this usually ended not in Gwen helping Clarissa, but the other way round!

Their beds were next to each other's at night, for Gwendoline had persuaded soft-hearted Mary-Lou to change beds with her, so that she might be next to Clarissa.

"She's never been to school before, you see, Mary-Lou," she said, "and as I hadn't either, before I came here, I do understand how she feels. It's at night you feel things worst. I'd like to be near her just to say a few words till she settles down properly."

Mary-Lou thought it was extraordinary of Gwendoline to develop such a kind heart all of a sudden, but she felt that it ought to be encouraged anyway – so she changed beds, and to Darrell's annoyance one night, there was Gwendoline next to Clarissa, whispering away like anything.

"Who told you you could change beds?" she demanded.

"Mary-Lou," said Gwendoline, in a meek voice.

"But – why in the world did you ask *Mary-Lou*?" said Darrell. "I'm the one to ask, surely."

"No. Because it was Mary-Lou's bed I wanted to change over, Darrell," explained Gwen, still in a meek voice. She saw that Darrell was annoyed, and decided to offer to change back again. Then surely Darrell would say all right, keep next to Clarissa!

"But, of course, if you'd rather I didn't sleep next to Clarissa – though I only wanted to *help* her—" said Gwendoline, in a martyr-like voice.

"Oh, stay there," said Darrell, who could never bear it when Gwendoline put on her martyr act. So Gwendoline, rejoicing inwardly, did stay there, and was able to whisper what she thought were comforting words to Clarissa at night. She was too far away from Darrell's bed to be heard – and in any case Darrell, usually tired out with work and games, went to sleep very quickly, and heard nothing.

Clarissa thought Gwendoline was really the kindest girl she had ever met – not that she had met many,

59

however! Feeling lonely and strange, she had welcomed Gwendoline's friendliness eagerly. She had listened to endless tales about Gwendoline's uninteresting family, who all seemed to be "wonderful" according to Gwen, and yet appeared to the listening Clarissa to be uniformly dull!

She said very little about her own family, though Gwendoline questioned her as much as she dared, longing to hear of Rolls Royces and yachts and mansions. But Clarissa merely spoke of their little country house, and their "car" – not even "cars", thought the disappointed Gwendoline.

As Clarissa had a weak heart, and did no games or gym, she hadn't much chance to get together with the other girls. She either had to rest at these times, or merely go to watch, which she found rather boring. So she looked forward eagerly to the times she could be with Gwendoline, who was practically her only companion.

That is, till Darrell really took the matter in hand! Seeing Gwendoline's fair head and Clarissa's auburn one bent together over a jigsaw puzzle one fine evening, when everyone should have been out of doors, she made up her mind that something really must be done!

She went to Mavis. After all, Mavis had no real friend, she just made a threesome with Daphne and Mary-Lou. She could quite well spare some of her time for Clarissa.

"Mavis," said Darrell, "we think that Clarissa is seeing a bit too much of darling Gwendoline Mary. Will you try and get Clarissa to yourself a bit and talk to her?"

Mavis was surprised and pleased. "Yes, of course, Darrell," she said. "I'd love to." Secretly she thought that the small, bespectacled Clarissa was quite well paired off with Gwendoline – but if Darrell thought otherwise, then it must be so! So obediently she went to try to prise Clarissa away from the close-clinging Gwen.

"Come down to the pool with me, Clarissa," she said, smiling pleasantly. "I'm not bathing today – but we'll go and watch the others. They want someone to throw in pennies for them to dive for."

Clarissa got up at once. Gwendoline frowned. "Oh, Clarissa – you can't go just yet."

"Why? We've nothing much to do," said Clarissa, surprised. "You come, too."

"No. I feel rather tired," said Gwendoline, untruthfully, hoping that Clarissa would stay with her. But she didn't. She went off with Mavis, rather flattered at having been asked by her. Clarissa had not much opinion of herself. She thought herself dull and plain and uninteresting, and indeed she certainly appeared so to most of the girls!

Darrell beamed at Mavis. Good old Mavis! She was doing her best, thought Darrell, pleased. But poor Clarissa didn't have much of a time with Gwendoline afterwards!

Gwendoline was rather cold, and gave her very short, cool answers when she returned from the pool. Clarissa was puzzled.

"I say – you didn't really mind my going off with Mavis for a bit, did you?" she said at last.

Gwendoline spoke solemnly. "Clarissa, you don't know as much about Mavis as I do. She's not the sort of girl your family would like you to be friends with. Do you know what she did last year? She heard of a talent-spotting competition in a town near here – you know, a very *common* show with perfectly dreadful people in it – and she actually went off by herself to sing in the show!"

Clarissa was truly horrified, partly because she knew that she herself would never have had the courage even to think of such a thing.

"What happened?" she said. "Tell me."

"Well – Mavis missed the last bus home," said Gwendoline, still very solemn. "And Miss Peters found her lying by the road at about three o'clock in the morning. After that she was terribly ill, and lost her voice. She thought she had a wonderful voice before that, you know – though I can't say *I* ever thought much of it – and so it was a very good punishment for her to lose it."

"Poor Mavis," said Clarissa.

"Well, personally I think she ought to have been expelled," said Gwendoline. "I've only told you this, Clarissa, because I want you to see that Mavis isn't really the kind of person to make friends with – that is if you were thinking of it."

"Oh no, I wasn't," said Clarissa, hastily. "I only just went down to the pool with her, Gwen. I won't even do that if you don't want me to."

Poor weak Clarissa had said just what Gwendoline hoped she would say, and the next time that Mavis came to ask her to go for a short walk with her, she refused.

"Don't bother Clarissa," said Gwendoline. "She really doesn't want you hanging round her."

The indignant Mavis walked away and reported to Darrell that *she* wasn't going to bother about that silly little Clarissa any more! She had better find someone else. What about Daphne?

Daphne came by at that moment and heard her name. In a fit of annoyance Darrell told her that Mavis had been rebuffed by Clarissa, and that Mavis had suggested that she, Daphne, should have a try. What about it?

"I don't mind having a shot – just to spoil darling Gwendoline Mary's fun," said Daphne with a grin. So she tried her hand at Clarissa, too, only to be met with excuses and evasions. Gwendoline had quite a bit to tell Clarissa about Daphne, too!

"You see, Clarissa," said Gwendoline, "Daphne isn't really *fit* to be at a school like this. You mustn't repeat what I tell you – but a year or two ago Daphne was found out to be a thief!"

Clarissa stared at Gwendoline in horror. "I don't believe it," she said.

"Well, just as you like," said Gwen. "But she *was* a thief – she stole purses and money and brooches – and this wasn't the only school she'd stolen at, either. When it was found out, Miss Grayling made her come into our common room, and confess everything to us – and we had to decide whether or not she should be expelled. It's as true as I'm standing here!"

Clarissa was quite pale. She looked across the court-yard to where Daphne was laughing with Mary-Lou. She couldn't believe it – and yet Gwendoline would never, never dare to tell such a lie as that.

"And – did you all say that – you didn't want her expelled?" she said at last.

"Well, *I* was the first to say she should have a chance and I'd stick by her," said Gwen, untruthfully, for it had been little Mary-Lou who had said that, not Gwen. "So she was kept on – but as you can see, Clarissa, she wouldn't be a really *nice* friend to have, would she? You'd never feel you could trust her."

"No. I suppose not," said Clarissa. "Oh, dear – I hate thinking nasty things about Mavis and Daphne like this. I hope there are no more nasty tales to tell."

"Did you ever hear how Darrell slapped me about a dozen times in the swimming pool, for nothing at all?" said Gwen, who had never forgotten or forgiven this episode. "I had a bad leg for ages after that. And you know that girl in the fifth – Ellen? Well, she tried to get hold of the exam papers and cheat by looking at the questions, the night before the exam! She did, really."

"Don't," said Clarissa, beginning to think that Malory Towers was a nest of cheats, thieves and idiots.

"And even Bill, whom everyone thinks such a lot of, was in awful disgrace last year, through continual deceit and disobedience," went on the poisonous voice in Clarissa's ear. "Do you know, Miss Peters had to threaten to send Bill's horse, Thunder, away to her home, because she was so disobedient?"

"I don't want to hear any more," said Clarissa, unhappily. "I really don't."

"Well, it's all true," said Gwendoline, forgetting her own record of deceit and unkindness, and not even realizing how she had distorted the facts, so that though most of them were capable of simple and kindly explanations, she had presented them as pictures of real badness.

Darrell came up, determined to get Clarissa away from Gwendoline's everlasting whispering. "Hey, Clarissa," she called, in a jolly voice. "You're just the person I'm looking for! Come and help me to pick some flowers for our classroom will you?"

Clarissa sat as if rooted to the spot. "Come on!" called Darrell, impatiently. "I shan't bite you – or even slap you!"

"Oh, dear!" thought Clarissa, getting up slowly, and remembering Gwen's tale of the dozen slaps Darrell had given her, "I hope she *doesn't* go for me!"

"Has dear Gwendoline been regaling you with tales of our dark, dreadful deeds?" said Darrell, and then, as she saw Clarissa go red, she knew that she had hit the nail on the head.

"Bother Gwendoline!" she thought. "She really is a poisonous little snake!"

A Day Off!

Three or four weeks went by. The School Certificate girls worked very hard indeed, and some of them began to look rather pale. Miss Williams decided it was time to slack off for a bit.

"Go for an all-day picnic," she suggested. "Go to Langley Hill and enjoy yourselves."

Langley Hill was a favourite spot for picnics. It was a lovely walk there, along the cliff, and from the top there was a magnificent view of the countryside and the sea.

"Oh thanks, Miss Williams! That would be super!" said Darrell.

"Smashing!" said Alicia, which was the favourite adjective of all the first-formers at the moment, often ridiculed by the older girls.

"Langley Hill," said Clarissa. "Why, that's where my old nurse lives!"

"Write and ask her if we could go and have tea with her," said Gwendoline, who didn't like what she called "waspy picnics" at all. "It would be nice for her to see you."

"You always think of such kind things, Gwendoline," said Clarissa. "I certainly will write. She will get us a wizard tea, I know. She's a marvellous cook."

So she wrote to her old nurse, who lived at the foot of Langley Hill. ("Thank goodness we shan't have to walk all the way up the hill with the others!" thought Gwendoline, thankfully. "I really am getting very clever!")

Old Mrs Lucy wrote back at once. "We're to go to her for tea," said Clarissa. "She says she'll have a real spread. What fun!"

"We'd better ask permission," said Gwendoline, suddenly thinking that Darrell might prove obstinate if the idea was suddenly sprung on her on the day of the picnic. "Go and ask Miss Williams, Clarissa."

"Oh no – you go," said Clarissa, who was always scared of asking any mistress anything. But Gwendoline knew better than to ask a favour of Miss Williams. Miss Williams saw right through Gwendoline, and might say "No" just on principle, if Gwen went to ask her a favour! She didn't trust Gwendoline any farther than she could see her.

So Clarissa had to go – and with many stammerings and stutterings she at last came out with what she wanted to ask – and handed over her old nurse's invitation.

"Yes. You can go there for tea, so long as you take another girl with you," said Miss Williams, thinking what an unattractive child Clarissa was, with her thick-lensed glasses and the wire round her teeth. She couldn't help looking so plain, of course – but that dreadful hangdog expression she always wore made it worse!

The day of the picnic dawned bright and clear, and promised to be lovely and hot.

"A whole day off!" rejoiced Darrell. "And such a day, too! I vote we take our bathing things and bathe at the foot of Langley Hill. There's a cove there."

"You'll have to take your lunch with you, but you

66

can have your tea at the little tea place on top of the hill," said Miss Williams. "I've asked the kitchen staff to let you go and help them cut sandwiches and cakes to take with you. Be off with you now – and come back ready to work twice as hard!"

They clattered off, and in half an hour were streaming up the cliff-path on their way to Langley Hill, each girl carrying her share of the lunch.

"I should think we've got far too much," said Mavis.

"*Do* you? I don't think we've got enough!" said Darrell, astonished. "But then, my idea of a good picnic lunch is probably twice the size of yours, Mavis! You're a poor eater."

Gwendoline and Clarissa panted along a good way behind the others. Darrell called to them to hurry up. She was annoyed to see the two together again after all her efforts to separate them.

"Clarissa gets a bad heart if she hurries," called Gwendoline, reproachfully. "You know that, Darrell."

"Oh, Gwen – I hardly ever feel my heart this term," said Clarissa. "I believe I'm almost cured! I can easily hurry."

"Well," said Gwendoline, solemnly, "I'm just a *bit* worried about *my* heart, Clarissa. It's done funny things lately. Sort of flutters like a bird, you know."

Clarissa looked alarmed. "Oh, Gwen – that's just what mine used to do. You'll have to be careful. Oughtn't you to see a doctor?"

"Oh no, I don't think so," said Gwen, bravely. "I hate going to Matron about anything. She makes such a fuss. And she's quite likely not to believe what I say. She's very hard, you know."

Clarissa had been to Matron once or twice, and had thought her very kind and understanding. She didn't know that Gwendoline had tried to stuff Matron up with all kinds of tales, term after term, whenever she wanted to get out of anything strenuous, and that Matron now consistently disbelieved anything that Gwendoline had to say. She merely handed out large doses of very disgusting medicine, no matter what Gwen complained of. In fact, Alicia said that she kept a special large bottle labelled "Medicine for Gwen" on the top shelf of her cupboard, a specially nasty concoction made up specially for malingerers!

"Look at Connie," said Gwen, as they gradually came nearer to the others. "Carrying Ruth's bag for her as well as her own! How can Ruth put up with it?"

"Well, they're twins," said Clarissa. "I expect they like to do things for each other. Let's catch them up and talk to them."

But the conversation as usual was carried on by Connie, not by Ruth!

"What a heavenly day for a picnic!" said Clarissa, looking at Ruth.

"Beautiful," said Connie, and began to talk about the food in the bags she carried.

Gwen spoke to Ruth. "Did you find the pencil you lost – that silver one?" she asked.

Connie answered for her as usual. "Oh yes – it was at the back of her desk after all."

"Ruth, look at that butterfly!" said Clarissa, determined to make Ruth speak. Whatever is it?"

"It's a fritillary, pearl-bordered," answered Connie, before Ruth had even got a look at the lovely thing. Then Gwen and Clarissa gave it up. You just couldn't get Ruth to speak before Connie got her word in.

They had the picnic in sight of Langley Hill, because they were much too hungry to wait till they had climbed up to the top. Gwendoline was very thankful. She was already puffing and blowing.

"You're too fat, that's what's the matter with you,

Gwendoline," said Alicia, unsympathetically. "Gosh, what a wonderful scowl you've put on now – one of your best. A real snooty scowl!"

Belinda overheard and rolled over to be nearer to them. She gazed at Gwendoline, and felt all over herself for her small sketchbook, which was always somewhere about her person.

"Yes – it's a peach of a scowl," she said, "a smasher! Hold it, Gwen, hold it! I *must* add it to my collection!"

Clarissa, Ruth and Connie looked surprised. "A collection of *scowls*?" said Connie. "I never heard of *that* before!"

"Yes, I've got a nice little bookful of all Gwendoline's different scowls," said Belinda. "The one that goes like this" – and she pulled a dreadful face – "and this one – and this one you must have seen hundreds of times!" She pulled a variety of faces, and everyone roared. Belinda could be very funny when she liked.

"Oh quick – Gwen is scowling again!" she said, and flipped open her little book. "You know, one term I stalked Gwen the whole time, waiting for her scowls, but she got wise to me the next term, and I hardly collected a single one. I'll show you my collection when I get back if you like, Clarissa."

"Er – well – I don't know if Gwen would like it," she began.

"Of course she wouldn't," said Belinda. Her quick pencil moved over the paper. She tore off the page and gave it to Clarissa.

"There you are – there's your darling Gwendoline Mary," she said. Clarissa gasped. Yes – it was Gwen to the life – and looking unpleasant, too! Wicked Belinda – her malicious pencil could catch anyone's expression and pin it down on paper immediately.

Clarissa didn't know what in the world to do with

the paper – tear it up and offend Belinda – or keep it and offend Gwendoline. Fortunately the wind solved the problem for her by suddenly whipping it out of her fingers and tossing it over the hedge. She was very relieved.

It was a lovely picnic. There were sandwiches of all kinds, buns, biscuits and slices of fruit cake. The girls ate every single thing and then lazed in the sun. Darrell reluctantly decided at three o'clock that if they were going to have tea at the top of Langley Hill, and bathe afterwards, they had better go now.

"Oh, Darrell – Clarissa and I have been given permission by Miss Williams to go and have tea with Clarissa's old nurse, Mrs Lucy, who lives at the foot of the hill," said Gwendoline, in the polite voice she used when she knew she was saying something that the other person was going to object to.

"Well! This is the first I've heard of it!" said Darrell. "Why ever couldn't you say so before? I suppose it's *true*? You're not saying this just to get out of climbing Langley Hill and bathing afterwards?"

"Of course not," said Gwendoline, with enormous dignity. "Ask Clarissa!"

Clarissa, feeling rather nervous of Darrell, produced the invitation from Mrs Lucy. "All right," said Darrell, tossing it back. "*How* like you, Gwen, to get out of a climb and a bathe! Jolly clever, aren't you!"

Gwendoline did not deign to reply, but looked at Clarissa as if to say "What a head girl! Disbelieving us like that!"

The girls left Gwen and Clarissa and went to climb the great hill. The two left behind sprawled on the grass contentedly. "I'm just as pleased not to climb that hill, anyway," said Gwen. "This hot afternoon, too! I wish them joy of it!"

They sat a little longer, then Gwen decided that

she was being bitten by something. She always decided this when she wanted to make a move indoors! So they set off to find Mrs Lucy's cottage, and arrived about a quarter past four.

The old lady was waiting. She ran out to greet Clarissa, and petted her as if she was a small child. Then she saw Gwendoline, and appeared to be most astonished that there were no other girls besides.

"But I've got tea for twenty!" she said. "I thought the whole *class* was coming, Miss Clarissa dear! Oh my, what shall we do? Can you go after the others and fetch them?"

An Exciting Plan

"You go after them, Gwen," said Clarissa, urgently. "I daren't tear up that steep hill. They'll be halfway up by now."

"No, indeed, Miss Clarissa, I wouldn't dream of *you* racing up that hill, and you only just recovering from that bad heart of yours," said Mrs Lucy at once. "I meant this other girl to go."

Gwendoline was certainly not going to go chasing up Langley Hill in the hot sun, to fetch back people she disliked, to enjoy a fine tea. Let them go without!

She pulled rather a long face. "I will go, of course," she said, "but I think there's something a bit wrong with *my* heart, too – it flutters, you know, when I've done something rather energetic. It makes me feel I simply must lie down."

"Oh dear – that's how I used to feel!" cried Clarissa,

sympathetically. "I forgot you spoke about your heart today, Gwen. Well, it can't be helped. We can't get the others back here to tea."

"What a pity," mourned Mrs Lucy, and took them inside her dear little cottage. Set on a table inside was a most marvellous home-made tea!

There were tongue sandwiches with lettuce, hard-boiled eggs to eat with bread and butter, great chunks of new-made cream cheese, potted meat, ripe tomatoes grown in Mrs Lucy's brother's greenhouse, ginger-bread cake fresh from the oven, shortbread, a great fruit cake with almonds crowding the top, biscuits of all kinds and six jam sandwiches!

"Gracious!" said Gwen and Clarissa, in awe. "What a spread!"

"Nurse, it's too marvellous for words," said Clarissa. "But oh dear, what a waste! And such an expense, too!"

"Oh now, you needn't think about that," said Mrs Lucy at once. "Your sister came to see me yesterday, her that's married, and she gave me some money to spend on getting a good spread for you all. So here it is – and only the two of you to eat it. Well, certainly, Miss Clarissa, you did give me to understand in your letter that the whole class were coming."

"No, Nurse – I said the whole of our form from North Tower were coming for a picnic and could we (that's Gwen and I) come and have tea with you," explained Clarissa. "I suppose you thought that 'we' meant the whole lot. I'm so very sorry."

"Sit you down and eat," said Mrs Lucy. But even with such a wonderful spread the two girls could not eat very much after their very good lunch. Gwen looked at the masses of food in despair.

And then Mrs Lucy had a brainwave.

"Don't you have midnight feasts or anything like

73

that at your school?" she said to Clarissa. "I remember your sister, her that's married, used to tell of them when *she* went to boarding school."

"A midnight feast!" said Gwen, remembering the one or two she had enjoyed at Malory Towers. "My *word*, that's a *super* idea, Mrs Lucy! Could we really have the food for that?"

"Of course you can. Then it will get to the hungry mouths it was made for," said old Mrs Lucy, her eyes twinkling at the two girls. "But how will you take it?"

Clarissa and Gwen considered. There was far too much for them to carry by themselves. They would simply *have* to have help. Clarissa was very excited. A midnight feast! She had read of such things – and now she was going to join in one – and provide the food, too!

"I know," said Gwen, suddenly. "We have to meet Darrell and the others at half past five, at the end of the lane down there – the one that leads up from the cove. We will bring some of the girls back here to help to carry the stuff!"

"Good idea," agreed Clarissa, her eyes shining behind their thick glasses. So, just before half past five by Mrs Lucy's clock, Gwen and Clarissa slipped along to the end of the lane to meet the others.

But only two were there – and very cross the two were. They were Alicia and Belinda.

"Well! Do you know it's a quarter to six, and we've jolly well been waiting for you two for twenty minutes!" began Alicia indignantly. "The others have gone on. We've had to wait behind. Haven't you got watches?"

"No," said Gwendoline. "I'm so sorry. I'm afraid Mrs Lucy's clock must have been slow."

"Well, for goodness' sake, put your best foot forward now," grumbled Alicia.

But Gwen caught at her arm.

"Wait a bit, Alicia. We want you and Belinda to come back to Mrs Lucy's cottage with us. It isn't far."

Alicia and Belinda stared in exasperation at Gwen. Rapidly she told them about the feast, and all the food left over – and how Mrs Lucy had offered it to them for a midnight feast.

A grin appeared on Alicia's face, and a wicked look on Belinda's. A midnight feast! That would be a fine end to a very nice day. All that food, too! It simply couldn't be wasted.

"Well, it would certainly be a sin to let all that wonderful food go stale," said Alicia, cheerfully. "I quite see you couldn't allow that. And I'm sure we could all do with a feast tonight, after our walking, climbing and bathing. We'll go back and help you carry the stuff."

No more was said about being late. The four of them went quickly back to Mrs Lucy's cottage. She had packed it up as best she could in net bags and baskets. The girls exclaimed in delight and thanked her heartily.

"We'll bring back the baskets and bags as soon as we can," promised Clarissa. "My, what a load we've got!"

They had indeed. It was all the four could do to lug it back to Malory Towers. Sally was waiting for them as they came down the cliff-path. "Whatever *have* you been doing?" she asked. "Darrell's in an awful wax, thinking you'd got lost or something. She was just about to go and report that you'd all fallen over the cliff!"

Alicia laughed. "Take a look at this basket," she said. "And this bag! Clarissa's old nurse gave us the whole lot for a midnight feast!"

"Golly!" said Sally, thrilled. "How super! You'd

75

better hide the things somewhere. We don't want Potty or Mam'zelle finding them."

"Where shall we put them?" wondered Alicia. "And where shall we have the feast! It would be better to have it out of doors tonight, it's so hot. I know! Let's have it down by the pool. We might even have a midnight swim!"

This sounded absolutely grand. "You go and tell Darrell we're safe," said Alicia, "and we four will slip down to the pool, and hide these things in the cubby holes there where we keep the lifebelts and things."

Sally sped off, and Gwen, Clarissa, Alicia and Belinda swiftly made their way down to the pool. The tide was out – but at midnight it would be in again, and they could splash about in the pool, and have their feast with the waves running over their toes. The moon was full, too – everything was just right!

Alicia packed the food into a cubby hole and shut the door. Then she and the others went up the cliff path, but halfway up Alicia remembered that she hadn't locked the door of the cubby hole she had used.

"Blow!" she said. "I suppose I'd better, in case anyone goes snooping round. You go on, you three – and I'll come as soon as I've locked up."

She went down and locked the cubby hole, slipping the key into her pocket. She heard footsteps near her as she pocketed the key and turned round hastily.

Thank goodness it was only Betty, her West Tower friend! "Hallo! What are you doing here?" said Betty.

Alicia grinned and told her about the hoard of food. "Why don't you ask *me* to come along?" said Betty. "Any objection?"

"No. It's just that Darrell mightn't like it," said Alicia, hesitating. "You know that we aren't supposed

76

to leave our towers and join up together at night. That's always been a very strict rule."

"Well – is there anything to stop me from looking out of my dormy window, hearing something going on at the pool, and coming along to see what it is?" said Betty, with her wicked grin. "Then I don't see how you can prevent everyone from saying, 'Come along and join us'."

"Yes – that's a wizard idea," said Alicia. "You do that. Then nobody will know I told you! I'll call out, 'Come and join us,' and that will make everyone else join in – and Darrell won't be able to say no!"

"Right," said Betty, and chuckled. "I could do with a spree like this, couldn't you? Where did you go today? Langley Hill? We went to Longbottom, and had some good fun. I say – I suppose I couldn't bring one or two more West Tower girls with me, could I? After all, it's not like being *invited* if we just pop along to see what the noise is. No one will ever know."

"All right. Bring Eileen and Winnie," said Alicia. "They'll enjoy it. But for goodness' sake don't say I told you, or Darrell will blow my head off! She's taking her head girl's duties very, very seriously!"

"She would!" said Betty, and laughed. "Well, see you tonight – and mind you're *very* surprised when we appear!"

She sped off and Alicia went to join the others. "Whatever made you so long?" demanded Belinda. "We thought you must have thrown a fit and fallen into the pool. You'll be late for supper now if you aren't quick."

"Have you told Darrell about the food and the midnight feast?" asked Alicia.

"Yes," said Belinda. "She looked a bit doubtful at first, and then when we reminded her that the great

77

Fifth had had one last term, she laughed and said, 'All right! A feast it shall be then!' "

"Good for Darrell," said Alicia, pleased. "Did you suggest that down by the pool would be a good place?"

"Yes. She agreed that it would," said Belinda. "So we're all set!"

The Upper Fourth winked at one another so continually that supper time that Mam'zelle, who was taking the supper table, looked down at her person several times to see if she had forgotten some article of apparel. Had she lost a few buttons? Was her belt crooked? Was her hair coming down? Then why did these bad girls wink and wink?

But it was nothing to do with Mam'zelle or her clothing or hair – it was just that the girls were thrilled and excited, and full of giggles and nudges and winks, enough to drive any mistress to distraction.

Mam'zelle was indulgent. "They are excited after their picnic," she thought. "Ah, how well they will sleep tonight!"

But Mam'zelle was wrong. They didn't intend to sleep at all well that night!

That Evening

"For goodness' sake don't let Potty or Mam'zelle guess there's anything planned for tonight," said Darrell to the others after supper. "I saw Mam'zelle looking very suspicious. Come into the common room now, and we'll arrange the details. How gorgeous to have so much food given to us – Clarissa, many thanks!"

Clarissa blushed, but was too nervous to say anything. She was delighted to think that she could provide a feast for the others.

They all went to the common room and sat about to discuss their plans. "It's such a terrifically hot evening that it really will be lovely down by the pool," said Sally. "There won't have to be any of the usual screeching or yelling though – sounds carry so at night, and although the pool is right down on the rocks, it's quite possible to hear noises from there if the wind is right."

Alicia was pleased to hear Sally say this. It would make it seem natural for Betty and Eileen and Winnie to come and say they had heard sounds from the pool.

"I and Sally will keep awake tonight," planned Darrell. "Then when we hear the clock strike twelve, we will wake you all, and you can get into dressing gowns and bring your bathing things. We'd better fetch them from the changing rooms now, or else we may wake up one of the staff, if we rummage about late at night."

"Is all the food safely down by the pool?" asked Bill, who was very much looking forward to this adventure. It was the first time she had ever been to a midnight feast!

"Yes. Safely locked in the cubby hole on the left," said Alicia. "I've got the key."

"We'll have a bathe first and then we'll feast," said Darrell. "It's a pity we haven't anything exciting to drink."

"I bet if I went and asked old Cookie for some lemonade, she'd leave us some ready," said Irene, who was a great favourite with the kitchen staff.

"Good. You go then," said Darrell. "Ask her to make two big jugfuls, and stand them on the cold larder floor. We'll fetch them when we're ready."

Irene sped off. Then Alicia was sent with Mavis to fetch the bathing things from the changing room. Everyone began to feel tremendously excited. Clarissa could hardly keep still.

"I wish I hadn't had so much supper," said Gwendoline. "I'm sure I shan't feel hungry by midnight."

"Serves you right for being a pig," said Belinda. "You had five tomatoes at supper. I counted!"

"A pity you hadn't anything better to do," said Gwendoline, trying to be sarcastic.

"Oh, it's wonderful to watch your nice little ways," said Belinda, lazily. "No wonder you're getting so fat, the way you gobble everything at meals. Dear me, what a wonderful drawing I could make of you as a nice fat little piggy-wig with blue eyes and a ribbon on your tail."

Everyone roared. "Do, do!" begged Sally. Gwendoline began to scowl, saw Belinda looking at her, and hastily straightened her face. She wished she hadn't tried to be sarcastic to Belinda. She always came off badly if she did!

Alicia and Mavis came back, giggling, with the bathing things. "Anyone spot you?" asked Darrell, anxiously.

"I don't think so. That pestiferous young cousin of mine, June, was somewhere about, but I don't think she'd spot anything was up," said Alicia. "I heard her whistling somewhere, when we were in the changing room."

Irene came back from the kitchen, grinning all over her face. "I found Cookie, and she was all alone," she said. "She'll have two thumping big jugs of lemonade ready for us on the floor of the larder, any time after eleven o'clock tonight. The staff go to bed then, so she says any time after that will be safe for us to get it. Whoops!"

"This is going to be super," said Alicia. "What exactly did you say the food was, Clarissa?"

Clarissa explained, with Gwen prompting her proudly. Gwen really felt as if she had provided half the feast herself, and she basked in Clarissa's reflected glory.

"Did you ever have midnight feasts at your last school, Ruth?" asked Darrell, seeing that Ruth looked as excited as the others.

Connie answered for her as usual. "No. We tried once, but we got caught – and my word we did get a wigging from the head."

"I asked Ruth, not you," said Darrell, annoyed with Connie. "Don't keep butting in. Let Ruth answer for herself." She turned to Ruth again.

"Was your last head very strict?" she asked. Connie opened her mouth to answer for Ruth again, caught the glint in Darrell's eye, and shut it.

Ruth actually answered, after waiting for a moment for Connie. "Well," she said, "I think probably *you* would call her very strict. You see . . ."

"Oh, not *very* strict, Ruth," interrupted Connie. "Don't you remember how nice she was over . . ."

"I'M ASKING RUTH," said Darrell, exasperated.

What would have happened next the form would dearly have loved to know – but there came an interruption that changed the subject. Matron popped her head in and said she wanted Gwendoline.

"Oh, *why*, Matron?" wailed Gwendoline. "What haven't I done now that I ought to have done? Why do you want me?"

"Just a little matter of darning," said Matron.

"But I've *done* the beastly darning you told me to," said Gwen, indignantly.

"Well then – shall we say a little matter of *un*picking and *re*-darning?" said Matron, aggravatingly. The girls

81

grinned. They had seen Gwen's last effort at darning a pair of navy-blue knickers with grey wool, and had wondered if Matron would notice.

Gwendoline had to get up and go, grumbling under her breath. "I could do her darning for her," suggested Clarissa to Darrell. "I don't play games or do gym – I've plenty of time."

"Don't you dare!" said Darrell at once. "You help her too much as it is – she's always copying from you."

Clarissa looked shocked. "Oh – she doesn't *copy*," she said loyally, going red at the idea of her daring to argue with Darrell.

"Don't be such a mutt," said Alicia, bluntly. "Gwendoline's a turnip-head – and she's always picked other people's brains and always will. Take off your rose-coloured glasses and see Gwen through your proper eyes, my dear Clarissa!"

Thinking that Alicia really *meant* her to take off her glasses for some reason, Clarissa removed her spectacles most obediently! The girls were about to laugh loudly, when Darrell bent forward in surprise.

"Clarissa! You've got real green eyes! I've never seen proper green eyes before! You must be related to the pixie folk – people with green eyes always are!"

Everyone roared – but on looking closely at Clarissa's eyes, they saw that they were indeed a lovely clear green, that somehow went remarkably well with her wavy auburn hair.

"My word – I wish I had stunning eyes like that," said Alicia enviously. "They're marvellous. How sickening that you've got to wear glasses."

"Oh, it's only for a time," said Clarissa, putting them on again, looking rather shy but pleased at Alicia's admiration. "I'm glad you like my green eyes! Gwendoline thinks it's awful to have green eyes like a cat."

"If all cats have green eyes, then our dear Gwendoline certainly ought to have them," said Belinda at once.

Clarissa looked distressed.

"Oh, but Gwendoline has been very kind to me," she began, and then everyone shushed her. Gwen was coming in at the door, scowling, holding a pair of games knickers and a pair of games stockings in her hands.

"I do think Matron's an absolute *beast*," she began. "I spent *hours* darning these last week – and now I've got to unpick all my darns and re-do them."

"Well, don't darn navy knickers with grey wool, or red stockings with navy wool this time," said Alicia. "Anyone would think you were colour blind."

Clarissa longed to help Gwen, but after Darrell's remark she didn't like to offer, and Gwen certainly didn't dare to ask for help. The girls sat about, yawning, trying to read, longing for bed because they really felt tired. But not too tired to wake up at twelve and have a bathe and a feast.

They didn't take long getting into bed that night. Even slow Gwendoline was quick. Irene was the quickest of the lot, much to Darrell's surprise. But it was discovered that she had absentmindedly got into bed half-undressed, so out she had to get again.

The bathing things were stacked in someone's cupboard, waiting. Dressing gowns and slippers were set ready on the ends of each bed.

"Sorry for you, Darrell, and you, too, Sally, having to keep awake till twelve!" said Irene, yawning. "Goodnight, all – see you in a little while!"

Sally said she would keep awake for the first hour, and then wake Darrell, who would keep awake till twelve. Then each would get a little rest.

Sally valiantly kept awake, and then shook Darrell,

who slept in the next bed. Darrell was so sound asleep that she could hardly open her eyes. But she did at last, and then decided she had better get out of bed and walk up and down a little, or she might fall off to sleep again – and then there would be no feast, for she was quite certain no one else would be awake at twelve!

At last she heard the clock at the top of the Tower striking twelve. Good. Midnight at last! She woke up Sally and then the two of them woke everyone else up. Gwendoline was the hardest to wake – she always was. Darrell debated whether or not to leave her, as she seemed determined not to wake – but decided that Clarissa might be upset – and after all, it was Clarissa's feast!

They all put on dressing gowns and slippers. They got their bathing things out of the cupboard and sent Irene and Belinda for the jugs of lemonade. The dormy was full of giggles and whisperings and shushings. Everybody was now wide awake and very excited.

"Come on – we'll go down to the side door, out into the garden, and through the gate to the cliff path down to the pool," whispered Darrell. "And for GOODNESS' sake don't fall down the stairs or do anything idiotic."

It wasn't long before they were down by the pool, which was gleaming in the moonlight, and looked too tempting for words. Irene and Belinda had the jugs of lemonade.

"Let's get out the food and have a look at it," said Sally. "I'm longing to see it!"

"Alicia! Where's the key of the cubby hole?" said Darrell.

"Blow!" said Alicia. "I've left it in my tunic pocket. I'll skip back and get it. Won't be half a minute!"

Midnight Feast!

Alicia ran up the cliff path, annoyed with herself for forgetting the key. She slipped in at the side door of the Tower and went up the stairs. As she went along the landing where the first-form dormy was, she saw a little white figure in the passage, looking out of the landing window.

"Must be a first-former!" thought Alicia. "What's she out at this time of night for? Little monkey!"

She walked softly up to the small person looking out of the window and grasped her by the shoulder. There was a loud gasp.

"Sh!" said Alicia. "Good gracious, it's *you*, June! What are you doing out here at midnight?"

"Well, what are *you*?" said June, cheekily.

Alicia shook her. "None of your cheek," she said. "Have you forgotten the trouncing I gave you last summer hols for cheeking me and Betty, when you came to stay with me?"

"No. I haven't forgotten," said June, vengefully. "And I never shall. You were a beast. I'd have split on you if I hadn't been scared. Spanking me with a hairbrush as if I was six!"

"Served you jolly well right," said Alicia. "And you know what would have happened to you if you *had* split – Sam and the others would have trounced you, too!"

"I know," said June, angrily. She was scared of Alicia's brothers. "You wait, though. I'll get even with you some time!"

Alicia snorted scornfully. "You could do with another spanking, I see," she said. "Now – you clear off to bed. You know you're not supposed to be out of your dormy at night."

"I saw you all go off with bathing things tonight," said June, slyly. "I guessed you were up to something, you fourth-formers, when I spotted you and somebody else getting bathing dresses in the changing room tonight. You thought I didn't see you, but I did."

How Alicia longed for a hairbrush to spank June with – but she dared not even raise her voice!

"Clear off to bed," she ordered, her voice shaking with rage.

"Are you having a midnight feast, too?" persisted June, not moving. "I saw Irene and Belinda with jugs of lemonade."

"Nasty little spy," said Alicia, and gave June a sharp push. "What we fourth-formers do is none of your business. Go to bed!"

June resisted Alicia's hand, and her voice grew dangerous. "Does Potty know about your feast?" she asked. "Or Mam'zelle? I say, Alicia, wouldn't it be rotten luck on you if somebody told on you?"

Alicia gasped. Could June really be threatening to go and wake one of the staff, and so spoil all their plans? She couldn't believe that anyone would be so sneaky.

"Alicia, let me come and join the feast," begged June. "Please do."

"No," said Alicia, shortly, and then, not trusting herself to say any more, she left June standing by the window and went off in search of the key to the cubby hole. She was so angry that she could hardly get the key out of her tunic pocket. To be cheeked like that by a first-former – her own cousin! To be

86

threatened by a little pipsqueak like that! Alicia really hated June at that moment.

She found the key and rushed back to the pool with it. She said nothing about meeting June. The others were already in the water, enjoying themselves.

"Pity the moon's gone in," said Darrell to Sally. "Gosh, it *has* clouded up, hasn't it? Is that Alicia back? Hey, Alicia, what a time you've been. Got the key?"

"Yes, I'm unlocking the cubby hole," called back Alicia. "Clarissa is here. She'll help me to get out the things. Pity it's so dark now – the moon's gone."

Suddenly, from the western sky, there came an ominous growl – thunder! Blow, blow, blow!

"Sounds like a storm," said Darrell. "I thought there might be one soon, it's so terrifically hot today. I say, Alicia, do you think we ought to begin the feast now, in case the storm comes on?"

"Yes," said Alicia. "Ah, there's the moon again, thank goodness!"

The girls clambered out of the water and dried themselves. As they stood there, laughing and talking, Darrell suddenly saw three figures coming down the cliff path from the school. Her heart stood still. Were they mistresses who had heard them?

It was Betty, of course, with Eileen and Winnie. The three of them stopped short of the pool and appeared to be extremely astonished to see such a gathering of the Upper Fourth.

"I say! Whatever are you doing?" said Betty. "We *thought* we heard a noise from the pool! It made us think that a bathe would be nice this hot night."

"We're going to have a feast!" came Alicia's voice. "You'd better join us."

"Yes, do – we've got plenty," said Irene, and the others called out the same. Even Darrell welcomed them, too, for it never once occurred to her that Betty had heard about the feast already and had come in the hope of joining them.

Neither did it occur to her that there was a strict rule that girls from one tower were never to leave their own towers at night to meet anyone from another. She just didn't think about it at all.

They all sat down to enjoy the feast. The thunder rumbled again, this time much nearer. A flash of lightning lit up the sky. The moon went behind an enormous cloud and was seen no more that night.

Worst of all, great drops of rain began to fall, plopping down on the rocks and causing great dismay.

"Oh dear – we'll have to go in," said Darrell. "We'll be soaked through, and it won't be any fun at all sitting and eating in the rain. Come on – collect the food and we'll go back."

Betty nudged Alicia. "Shall *we* come?" she whispered.

"Yes. Try it," whispered back Alicia. "Darrell hasn't said you're not to."

So everyone, including Betty, Eileen and Winnie from West Tower, gathered up the food hurriedly, and stumbled up the cliff path in the dark.

"Where shall we take the food?" panted Darrell to Sally. "Can't have it in our common room because it's got no curtains and the lights would shine out."

"What about the first-form common room?" asked Sally. "That's not near any staff room, and the windows can't be seen from any other part."

"Yes. Good idea," said Darrell, and the word went round that the feast was to be held in the first-form common room.

Soon they were all in there. Darrell shut the door carefully and put a mat across the bottom so that not a crack of light could be seen.

The girls sat about on the floor, a little damped

by the sudden storm that had spoilt their plans. The thunder crashed and the lightning gleamed. Mary-Lou looked alarmed, and Gwen went quite white. Neither of them liked storms.

"Hope Thunder's all right," said Bill, tucking into a tongue sandwich. Her horse was always her first thought.

"I should think . . ." began Alicia, when she stopped dead. Everyone sat still. Darrell put up her finger for silence.

There came a little knocking at the door. Tap-tap-tap-tap! Tap-tap-tap-tap!

Darrell felt scared. Who in the world was there? And why knock? She made another sign for everyone to keep absolutely still.

The knocking went on. Tap-tap-tap. This time it was a little louder.

Still the girls said nothing and kept quite silent. The knocking came again, sounding much too loud in the night.

"Oh dear!" thought Darrell, "if it gets any louder, someone will hear, and the cat will be out of the bag!"

Gwendoline and Mary-Lou were quite terrified of this strange knocking. They clutched each other, as white as a sheet.

"Come in," said Darrell, at last, in a low voice, when there was a pause in the knocking.

The door opened slowly, and the girls stared at it, wondering what was coming. In walked June – and behind her, rather scared, was Felicity!

"June!" said Alicia, fiercely.

"*Felicity!*" gasped Darrell, hardly believing her eyes.

June stared round as if in surprise.

"Oh," she said, "It's you, is it! Felicity and I simply *couldn't* get to sleep because of the storm, and we came to the landing window to watch it. And we found these on the ground!"

She held up three hardboiled eggs! "We were awfully surprised. Then we heard a bit of a noise in here and we wondered who was in our common room – and we thought whoever it was must be having a good old feast – so we came to bring you your lost hardboiled eggs."

There was a silence after this speech. Alicia was boiling! She knew that June had watched them coming back because of the storm – had seen them going into the first-form common room – and had been delighted to find the dropped eggs and bring them along as an excuse to join the party!

"Oh," said Darrell, hardly knowing what to say. "Thanks. Yes – we're having a feast. Er . . ."

"Why did you use our common room?" asked June, innocently, and she broke the shell off one of the eggs. "Of course, it's an honour for us first-formers to have you Upper Fourth using our room for a feast. I say – this egg's super! I didn't mean to nibble it, though. So sorry."

"Oh, finish it if you like," said Darrell, not finding anything else to say.

"Thanks," said June, and gave one to Felicity, who began to eat hers, too.

It ended, of course, in the two of them joining in the feast, though Darrell really felt very uncomfortable about it. Also, for the first time she realized that the three girls from West Tower were still there, in North Tower where they had no business to be! Still, how could she turn them out now? She couldn't very well say, "Look here, you must scram! I know we said join the feast when we were down by the pool – but we can't have you with us now." It sounded too silly for words.

Darrell did not enjoy the feast at all. She wanted to send June and Felicity away, but it seemed mean to do that when the feasters were using their common room, and June had brought back the eggs. Also she felt that Alicia might not like her to send June away. Little did she know that Alicia was meditating all kinds of dire punishments for the irrepressible June. Oh dear – the lovely time they had planned seemed to have gone wrong somehow.

And then it went even more wrong! Footsteps were heard overhead.

Things Happen Fast

"Did you hear that?" whispered Sally. "Someone is coming! Quick, gather everything up, and let's go!"

The girls grabbed everything near, and Darrell caught up the brush by the fireplace and swept the crumbs under a couch. She put out the light and opened the door. All was dark in the passage outside. There seemed to be nobody there. Who could have been walking about overhead? That was where the first-form dormy was.

June and Felicity were scared now. They shot away at once. Betty, Eileen and Winnie disappeared to the stairs, running down them to the side door. They could then slip round to their own tower. The others, led by Darrell, went cautiously upstairs to find their own dormy.

A slight cough from somewhere near, a familiar and unmistakable cough, brought them to a stop. They stood, hardly daring to breathe, at the top of the stairs. "That was Potty's cough," thought Darrell. "Oh blow – did she hear us making a row? But we really were quite quiet!"

She hoped and hoped that Betty and the other two West Tower girls had got safely to their own dormy without being caught. It really was counted quite a serious offence for girls of one tower to meet girls in another tower at night. For one thing there was no way to get from one tower to another under cover. The girls had to go outside to reach any other tower.

What could Potty be doing? Where was she? The girls stood frozen to the ground, waiting for the sign to move on.

"She's in the third-form dormy," whispered Darrell, at last. "Perhaps somebody is ill there. I think we had better make a dash for it, really. We can't stand here for hours."

"Right. The next time the thunder comes, we'll run for it," said Sally, in a low voice. The word was passing along, and the girls waited anxiously for the thunder. The lightning flashed first, showing up the crouching line of girls very clearly – and then the thunder came.

It was a good long, rumbling crash, and any sound the girls made in scampering along to their dormy was completely deadened. They fell into bed thankfully, each girl stuffing what she carried into the bottom of her cupboard, wet bathing suits and all.

No Miss Potts appeared, and the girls began to breathe more freely. Somebody *must* have been taken ill in the third-form dormy. Potty still seemed to be there. At last the Upper Fourth heard the soft closing of the third-form dormy door, and Miss Potts' footsteps going quietly off to her own room.

"Had we better take the lemonade jugs down to the kitchen now?" whispered Irene.

"No. We won't risk any more creeping about to-night," said Darrell. "You must take them down before breakfast, as soon as the staff have gone into the dining room, even though it makes you a bit late. And we'll clear out all the food left over before *we* go down, and hide it somewhere till we can get rid of it. *What* a pity that beastly storm came!"

The girls slept like logs that night, and could hardly wake up in the morning. Gwen and Belinda had to be literally *dragged* out of bed! Irene shot down to the kitchen with the empty jugs. All the rest of the food was hastily put into a bag and dumped into an odd cupboard in the landing. Then, looking demure and innocent, the fourth-formers went down to breakfast.

Felicity grinned at Darrell. She had enjoyed the escapade last night. But June did not grin at Alicia. Alicia's face was very grim, and June felt uncomfortable.

At Break Alicia went to find Hilda, the head girl of the first form. Hilda was surprised and flattered.

"Hilda," said Alicia, "I am very displeased with June's behaviour. She is getting quite unbearable, and we fourth-formers are not going to stand it. Either you must put her in her place, or we shall. It would be much better for you to do it."

"Oh, Alicia, I'm so sorry," said Hilda. "We *have* tried to put her in her place, but she keeps saying you'll give us no end of a wigging if we don't give her a chance. But we've given her lots of chances."

"I bet you have," said Alicia, grimly. "Now, I don't know how *you* deal with your erring form-members, Hilda – we had various very good ways when *I* was a first-former – but please do *some*thing – and tell her I told you to!"

"Right. We will," said Hilda, thankful that she had got authority to deal with that bumptious, brazen conceited new girl, June! A week of being sent to Coventry would soon bring June to heel – she loved talking and gossiping, and it would be a hard punishment for her. Hilda went off to call a form meeting about the matter, feeling very important.

June was angry and shocked to hear the verdict of her form – to be sent to Coventry for a week. She felt humiliated, too – and how angry she was with Alicia for giving Hilda the necessary authority! Alicia was quite within her rights to do this. When a member of a lower form aroused the anger or scorn of a higher form, the head girl of the offender's form was told to deal with the matter. And so Hilda dealt with it faithfully and promptly, and if she felt very pleased to do it, that was June's fault, and not hers. June was certainly a thorn in the side of all the old girls in the first form. It was quite unheard of for any new girl to behave so boldly.

Felicity found that she too had to give her promise not to speak to June. Oh dear – that would be very awkward – but she owed more loyalty to her form than to June. So she gave her promise in a low voice, not daring to look at the red-faced June.

That evening Felicity came to Darrell, looking worried. "Darrell, please may I speak to you? Something rather awful has happened. Those crumbs we left in the common room last night, under the couch, were found this morning, and so were two sandwiches. And Potty tackled Hilda and asked her if she'd been having a midnight feast there last night. Potty said she thought she heard something, but by the time she came out of the third-form dormy, where somebody was ill, and went to look in the common room, it was empty."

"Gosh," said Darrell. Then her face cleared. "Well, what's it matter? Hilda must have been asleep last night, and can't have known anything about it."

"She *was* asleep – and she told Potty she didn't know a thing about any feast, and that the first form certainly hadn't been out of the dormy last night," said Felicity. "Some of them woke up in that storm, but nobody missed me or June, apparently."

"Well, why worry then?" said Darrell. "You shouldn't have come along with June last night, you know, Felicity. I was awfully surprised and not at all pleased to see you. You really ought to be careful your very first term."

"I know," said Felicity. "I sort of get carried along by June. Honestly I can't help it, Darrell – she makes me laugh so much and she's so bold and daring. She's been sent to Coventry now, and she's as mad as anything. She knows it's all because of Alicia and she vows she'll get even with her. She will, too."

"Felicity – do chuck June," begged Darrell. "She's no good as a friend. She's a little beast, really. Alicia has told me all about her."

But Felicity was obstinate and she shook her head. "No. I like June and I want to stick by her. She's not a little beast. She's fun."

Darrell let Felicity go, feeling impatient with her little sister. Anyway, thank goodness Potty hadn't found out anything. She must be jolly puzzled about the crumbs and the sandwiches!

It seemed as if the whole affair would settle down – and then a bombshell came! Felicity came to Darrell again the next day, looking very harassed indeed.

"Darrell! I must speak to you in private."

"Good gracious! What's up now?" said Darrell, taking Felicity to a corner of the courtyard.

"It's June. I don't understand her. She says she's going to go to Potty and own up that she was at the midnight feast," said Felicity. "She says I ought to go and own up, too."

Darrell stared at Felicity in exasperation. These first-formers! "But if she goes and does that, it's as good as sneaking on *us*," said Darrell, furiously. "Where's this little pest now?"

"In one of the music rooms practising," said Felicity, alarmed at Darrell's fury. "She's in Coventry, you know, so I can't speak to her. She sent me a note. Whatever am I to do, Darrell? If she goes to own up, I'll *have* to go, too, or Potty and the rest will think I'm an awful coward."

"I'll go and talk to June," said Darrell, and went straight off to the music room, where the girls practised daily. She found June and burst into the room so angrily that the first-former jumped.

"Look here, June, what's behind this sudden piousness of yours – wanting to go and 'own up' – when there's no need for anything of the sort?" cried Darrell, angrily. "You know you'd get the Upper Fourth into trouble if you go and split."

"I shan't split," said June, calmly, playing a little scale up and down the piano. "I shall simply own up I was at THE feast – but I shan't say whose feast. I – er – want to get it off my conscience."

"You're a little hypocrite!" said Darrell. "Stop playing that scale and listen to me."

June played another little scale, a mocking smile on her face. Darrell nearly burst with rage. She slapped June's hand off the piano, and turned her round roughly to face her.

"Stop it," said June. "I've had enough of that kind of thing from my dear cousin Alicia!"

At the mention of Alicia's name, something clicked

97

into place in Darrell's mind, and she knew at once what was behind June's pious idea of "owning up". She wanted to get even with Alicia. She would like to get her into trouble – and Darrell too – and everyone in the Upper Fourth – to revenge herself on Alicia's order to Hilda to deal with her.

"You *are* a double-faced little wretch, aren't you?" said Darrell, scornfully. "You know jolly well if you 'own up' – pooh! – that Potty will make inquiries and *I* shall have to own up to the spree in the pool, and the feast afterwards."

"Oh – worse than that!" said June, in her infuriatingly impudent voice. "Girls from another tower were there – or was I mistaken?"

"Do you mean to say you'd split on Betty and the others, too," said Darrell, taking a deep breath, "just to get even with Alicia?"

"Oh – not *split* – or even *sneak*," said June, beginning to play the maddening scale again. "Surely I can own up – and Betty's name can – er – just *slip* out, as it were."

At the thought of June sneaking on everyone, under cover of being a good little girl and "owning up", Darrell really saw red. Her temper went completely, and she found herself pulling the wretched June off the piano stool and shaking her violently.

A voice made her stop suddenly.

"DARRELL! Whatever *are* you doing?"

A Real Shake-up

Darrell stared wildly round. Miss Potts stood at the door, a picture of absolute amazement. Darrell couldn't think of a word to say. June actually had the audacity to reseat herself on the piano stool and play a soft chord.

"June!" said Miss Potts, and the tone of her voice made the first-former almost jump out of her skin.

"Come with me, Darrell," said Miss Potts. "And you, too, June."

They followed her to her room, where Mam'zelle was correcting papers. She gazed in surprise at Miss Potts' grim face, and at the faces of the two girls.

"*Tiens!*" said Mam'zelle, gathering up her papers quickly, and beginning to scuttle out of her room. "I will go. I will not intrude, Miss Potts."

Miss Potts didn't appear to have noticed Mam'zelle at all. She sat down in her chair and looked sternly at Darrell and June.

"What were you two doing?"

Darrell swallowed hard. She was already ashamed of herself. Oh dear – head girl – and she had lost her temper like that! "Miss Potts – June has something to say to you," she said at last.

"What have you to say?" inquired Miss Potts, turning her cold eyes on June.

"Well, Miss Potts – I just wanted to own up that I had been to a midnight feast," said June.

"Hilda said that there had been no midnight feast,"

99

said Miss Potts, beginning to tap on the table with her pencil, always a danger sign with her.

"I know. It wasn't a first-form affair," said June smoothly.

"I gather from Darrell's face that it was a fourth-form affair," said Miss Potts.

Darrell nodded miserably. "Just the fourth-formers and you, June, I suppose?" said Miss Potts.

"Well – there were a few others," said June, pretending to hesitate. "One from my form as well as me. I won't mention her name."

"Felicity was there," said Darrell. "But I take responsibility for that. She didn't mean to come. And Miss Potts – Betty Hill, and Eileen and Winnie were there, too."

There was a silence. Miss Potts looked very grim.

"Girls from another tower?" she said. "I think you know the rule about that, don't you, Darrell? And what could you have been thinking about to invite two first-formers as well? Of course – Felicity is your sister – but surely . . ."

"I didn't invite her," said Darrell. "And – well – I didn't exactly invite the West Tower girls either."

"Don't let's quibble and make excuses," said Miss Potts, impatiently. "That isn't like you, Darrell. I imagine you were quarelling with June because she wanted to own up?"

Darrell couldn't trust herself to speak. She nodded. "I'm sorry I behaved like that," she said, humbly. "I thought I'd conquered my temper, but I haven't. I'm sorry I shook you, June."

June was a little taken aback at this apology, and looked uneasy. But she was very cock-a-hoop and pleased with herself. She was in Potty's good books for "owning up", she had got Darrell into trouble, and Alicia would get into trouble too and all the others – and she, June, would get off scot-free!

"You can go, June," said Miss Potts, suddenly. "I'm not sure I've got to the bottom of all this yet. Darrell had no right to use violence to you – but as she never loses her temper now unless something very serious makes her angry, I am inclined to take your 'owning-up' with a pinch of salt. You may be sure I shall find out whether you are to be praised or blamed!"

June shot out of the room, scared. Miss Potts looked gravely at Darrell. "Darrell, you know that you will have to bear the responsibility for allowing girls from another tower into your tower at night, don't you?" she said. "And I cannot possibly pass over your behaviour to June in the music room. Whatever provocation you had does not excuse what you did."

"I know," said Darrell, miserably. "I'm not a good head girl, Miss Potts. I'd better resign."

"Well – either you must resign, or you will have to be demoted," said Miss Potts, sadly. "Sally must be head for the time being – till we consider you can take the responsibility again. If you can't control yourself, Darrell, you certainly can't control others."

The news soon flew through the school. "Darrell Rivers has resigned as head girl! Did you know? There has been a most awful row – something about a midnight feast, and she actually asked girls from another tower – and first-formers as well. Gosh! Fancy *Darrell Rivers* getting into disgrace!"

Felicity heard the news and was filled with the utmost horror. She went straight to June, quite forgetting that she was still in Coventry.

"Did you go and split?" she asked, sharply. "What has happened?"

Full of glee at all that had happened, June told

Felicity the whole thing from beginning to end. "That will teach the fourth-formers to have a down on me and get me sent to Coventry," she said. "I've paid Alicia back nicely – and my word, you should have seen Darrell's face when she was shaking me, and Miss Potts came in and saw her. I'm glad she's not head girl of her form any longer. Serves her right!"

Felicity could hardly believe her ears. She was trembling, shivering all over. June noticed it with surprise.

"What's the matter?" she said. "You're my friend, aren't you?"

"I was. But have your forgotten that Darrell is my sister?" said Felicity, in a choking voice. June stared at her blankly. In her glee at being top dog she *had* completely and utterly forgotten that Darrell was Felicity's sister.

"I feel like Darrell – I could shake you and slap you, you horrid, two-faced beast!" cried Felicity. "As it is, I'm going to Hilda to tell her every single thing you've told me – that's not sneaking – that's reporting something almost too bad to be true! Ugh! You ought to be expelled. How could I *ever* have wanted you for a friend!"

And so the friendship between Felicity and June came to a most abrupt end, and was never renewed again. Susan was hunted out by Felicity and gave her the comfort she needed. June kicked herself for forgetting that Darrell was Felicity's sister; but the damage was done. Felicity had seen June in her true colours – and she didn't like them at all!

The fourth form were horrified at all that had happened. One and all they stood by poor Darrell, even Gwendoline coming to offer a few words of sympathy.

102

But Gwen's sympathy was, as usual, only on the surface. Immediately after she had been to tell Darrell how sorry she was, she was confiding to Clarissa that she really wasn't surprised that Darrell was in disgrace.

"I told you how she slapped me, didn't I," she said. "And she pushed Sally over once. It'll do her good to be humiliated like this. I never did like Darrell."

Clarissa looked at Gwendoline with a sudden feeling of dislike. "Why do you say this when you have just told her you're sorry, and that you'd do anything you could to put things right?" she said. "I think you're beastly, Gwen."

And to Gwen's unutterable surprise, the meek, weak Clarissa turned her back on her and walked away! It had cost her a great deal to say this to Gwen, and she was crying as she walked away.

She bumped into Bill, off to ride on Thunder. "Here, look where you're going, Clarissa. I say, you're crying. Whatever's up?" said Bill, in surprise.

"Nothing," said Clarissa, not wanting to say anything against Gwen.

Bill only knew one cure for unhappiness – riding a horse! She offered the cure to Clarissa now.

"Come for a ride. It's heavenly out now. You said you were allowed to ride if you wanted to. There's a horse free, I know. Miss Peters is coming, too. She's grand."

Another time Clarissa would have said no, because it was difficult for her to make up her mind to begin anything fresh, and she had not yet ridden at Malory Towers, although she had been told that she could. But now, touched by Bill's blunt kindliness, and feeling that she wanted to get right away from Gwendoline, she nodded her head.

"All right. I'll change into my jodhpurs quickly. Wait for me."

And in fifteen minutes' time, to Gwendoline's enormous surprise, Miss Peters, Bill – and *Clarissa* swept past her on the cliff, riding fast, shouting to one another as they went. *Clarissa*! Well! She hadn't even known that Clarissa had riding things with her. And there she was, off with that awful Bill and that even more awful Miss Peters! Gwendoline really couldn't understand it at all.

Sally was made temporary head girl. "I shall really *share* it with you," she told the subdued Darrell. "I shall come and ask you everything and take your advice – and I bet it won't be long before you're made head girl once more. Miss Grayling told me twice I was only temporary."

Darrell had written to her parents and told them the bad news. They would be sorry and upset, but they had to know. "I thought I must tell you before you come to see me and Felicity at half term," wrote Darrell. "Please don't say anything about it when you see me, will you, because I shall howl! Anyway, dears, one good thing has come out of all this – Felicity's not friends any more with the horridest girl in her form, but with one of the nicest – Susan, whom you saw at the gym display last term."

Darrell had been very touched by the sympathy given to her by her form. The twins had been very nice, she thought, even though Ruth, as usual, had not said a word – everything had been said by Connie. And as for Clarissa, she had been almost in tears when she came to Darrell.

"I believe Clarissa's awfully nice, when you can get under her meekness and shyness," said Darrell to Sally. "*What* a pity she has to wear those glasses! Didn't you think she looked beautiful when she took them off the other day – those deep green eyes, like water in a pool."

Sally laughed. "You sound quite poetical," she said. "Yes, I like Clarissa now. Gwen doesn't quite know what to think about Clarissa going off riding with Bill, does she? I never knew Clarissa was so fond of horses! She and Bill gabble like anything about all the horses they have ever known – and Gwendoline looks on like a dying duck in a thunderstorm, trying to get a word in."

"Half term next week," said Darrell. "Oh, Sally, I never dreamt when I was feeling so proud of being made head girl that I'd lose my position before even half term came. I'm a terrible failure!"

"Well – plenty of people would like to be the kind of failure *you* are!" said Sally, loyally. "You may be a failure at the moment – but you're a very *fine* failure. Darrell. You're a lot better than some people who think they're a success."

Gwendoline Makes a Plan

Half term would soon be coming! The school was giving all kinds of displays – an exhibition tennis match played by four of the crack school players – a swimming and diving display – and a dancing display in the middle of the great courtyard.

"And after that," said Daphne, gloomily, "after that – the School Cert. exam! I feel awfully depressed whenever I think of it."

"Think how lighthearted you'll be afterwards!" said Belinda.

"Yes – like you feel after going to the dentist,"

said Clarissa. "You get all gloomy beforehand and then after you've been you feel awfully happy."

Everyone laughed. They knew that Clarissa had had bad times at the dentist, and they knew that she hated the wire round her front teeth, put there to keep them back. She was hoping she could have it off before long.

"Once I've got rid of that wire and my glasses you won't know me!" she said, and shook back her mass of auburn hair.

She had been riding quite a bit with Bill, and Gwendoline had felt rather out of things. Clarissa rode extremely well, and could apparently manage any horse in the school stables – and had actually been permitted to try Thunder!

Gwendoline found the everlasting horse conversation between the two very trying indeed.

"I once rode a horse who ran away with me and jumped over a hedge before I had even learnt how to jump!" Clarissa would begin.

And then Bill would go on. "Did you really? I bet you stuck on all right. Did I ever tell you about Marvel, my brother Tom's horse?"

Then would follow a long story about Marvel. At the end Gwendoline would try to get a word in.

"I say – Clarissa, do you know where we are going for this afternoon's walk?"

"Not yet," Clarissa would say. "Well, Bill, I simply must tell you about my father's old horse that lived to be over thirty. He . . ."

And so the horsy conversation would go on, till Gwendoline felt she could scream. Horses! Horrible great snorting stamping creatures! How she wished Clarissa had never gone out for that first ride with Bill.

Gwendoline was beginning to be very much afraid

106

of the coming exam. She was backward in her lessons, and because of her habit of picking other people's brains, and of copying their work, her own brains worked very badly when she had to think out something for herself. The exam paper had to be done with her own brains – she couldn't copy anyone's work then – and indeed Gwen knew perfectly well that Miss Williams would see to it that she, Gwendoline, would be seated much too far away from anyone else to copy!

She worried about the exam. She felt uncomfortably that she might possibly be the only person to fail – and what a disgrace and humiliation that would be! Her father would have a lot of hurtful remarks to make, and her mother would cry, and her old governess would look mournful, and say it was all her fault, she ought to have taught Gwen better when she was small. Oh dear – why did these beastly exams matter?

Gwendoline seriously considered the possibility of trying to see the papers beforehand – but that was silly, she knew. They were always locked up. She did not think to herself, "I am *wrong* to think of such a thing," she merely thought, "I am silly to think there would be a chance of seeing them."

Could she be ill? Could she complain of a sore throat and headache? No – Matron simply *never* believed her. She would take her temperature and say, "My dear Gwendoline, you are suffering from inflammation of the imagination as usual," and give her that perfectly horrible medicine.

She thought of Clarissa's weak heart with envy. To have something like that – that prevented you from playing those awful games, and from swimming and climbing up hills – now that was something really worth while having – something sensible. Unfortunately, though, it didn't let you off lessons.

Gwendoline thought about weak hearts for a while, and gradually a plan began to unfold itself in her mind. What about putting it round that her heart was troubling her? She put her hand to where she thought her heart was, and assumed an agonized expression. What should she say? "Oh, my heart – it's fluttering again! I do wish it wouldn't. It makes me feel so odd. Oh, why did I run up those stairs so fast!"

The more she thought about this idea, the better it seemed. Next week was half term. If she could work up this weak heart business well enough, perhaps her parents would be told, and they would be alarmed and take her away home. Then she would miss School Cert. which began not long after!

Gwendoline's heart began to beat fast as she thought out this little plan. In fact, she felt a little alarmed, feeling it beat so fast with excitement. Suppose she really *had* got one? No – it was only that she was feeling excited about this clever and wonderful idea of hers.

So, little by little, Gwen began to put it about that she didn't feel very well. "Oh, nothing much," she told Clarissa and Bill. "*You'll* know what I feel like, Clarissa – my heart sort of *flutters*! Oh, why did I run up the stairs so fast?"

Clarissa was sympathetic. She knew how absolutely sickening a weak heart was. "Don't you think you ought to tell Miss Williams, or Miss Potts?" she said, quite anxiously. "Or Matron?"

"No," said Gwendoline, putting on a pathetically brave face. "I don't want to make a fuss. Besides, you know, it's School Cert. soon. I mustn't miss that."

If Alicia, Sally or Darrell had been anywhere near, they would have yelled with laughter at all this, but Bill and Clarissa didn't. They listened quite seriously.

"Well, *I* think you ought to say something about

it," said Clarissa. "If you'd had to go through what *I've* had to – lie up for weeks on end, not do a thing, give up all the riding and swimming I loved – you'd not run any risk of playing about with a groggy heart."

Gwendoline took to running up the stairs when she saw any of the Upper Fourth at the top. Then, when she came to the landing, she would put her hand to her left side, droop over the banisters and groan.

"Got a stitch?" Alicia would say, unsympathetically. "Bend down and touch your toes, Gwendoline. Oh – I forgot – you're too fat to do that, aren't you?"

On the other hand Mary-Lou might say, "Oh, Gwen, what's the matter? Is it your heart again? You really ought to have something done about it!"

Gwen did not perform in front of either Miss Williams or Miss Potts. She had a feeling that her performance would not go down very well. But she tried it on with Mam'zelle, who could always be taken in.

Mam'zelle was quite alarmed one morning to find Gwen sitting on the top stair near her room, her hand pressed to her heart, groaning.

"Ma petite, qu'as-tu fait? What is the matter?" she cried. "You have hurt yourself? Where?"

"It's – it's all right, Mam'zelle," panted Gwendoline. "It's – it's nothing – just this awful heart of mine. When I run or do anything energetic – it seems to go all funny!"

"You have the palpitations! You are anaemic then!" cried Mam'zelle. "Me, I once suffered in this way when I was fifteen! You shall come with me to Matron, and she shall give you some good, good medicine to make your blood rich and red."

Gwendoline didn't want her blood made "rich and red" by Matron. It was the last thing in the world she wanted! She got up hastily and smiled weakly at Mam'zelle.

"It's over now! I'm quite all right. It's not anaemia, Mam'zelle – I've never been anaemic. It's just my silly heart. It's – er – it's a weakness in our family, I'm afraid."

This was quite untrue, but Gwendoline added it because she thought it might convince Mam'zelle it was her heart and not her blood that was wrong! Mam'zelle was very sympathetic, and told Gwen she had better not play tennis that afternoon.

Gwendoline was delighted – but on thinking it over she regretfully decided that she had better play, because she wouldn't possibly be able to convince Sally that her heart had played her up again. Sally just simply didn't believe in Gwen's weak heart. So she played. Mam'zelle saw her and was surprised.

"The brave Gwendoline!" she thought. "She plays even though she knows it may bring on the palpitations again! Ah, these English girls, they have the courage and the pluck!"

Gwendoline laid a few more plans. She would bring Mam'zelle up to her parents at half term, and leave her to talk to them. She was certain that sooner or later Mam'zelle would speak about her heart – and then she, Gwen, would be anxiously questioned by her mother – and if she played her cards well, she would be taken home at once by a very anxious and frightened mother!

Gwen did not stop to think of the pain and anxiety she would give to her parents by her stupid pretence. She wanted to get out of doing the exam, and she didn't mind how she did it. She was quite unscrupulous, and very clever when she badly wanted her own way.

"I'm certain Mother will take me home," she thought. "I really don't think I need bother about swotting up for the exam. It will be a waste of time if I don't take it. Look at all the others – groaning and moaning every evening, mugging up Latin and French and maths and history and the rest! Well – *I* shan't!"

And, to the surprise of everyone, Gwendoline suddenly stopped working hard, and slacked!

"Aren't you afraid of doing frightfully bad papers?" asked Mavis, who was rather afraid of this herself, and was working very hard indeed.

"I shall do my best," said Gwendoline. "I can't do more. It's this beastly heart of mine, you know – it does play me up so, if I work too hard."

Mavis didn't believe in this heart of Gwendoline's, but she was really puzzled to know why the girl was so silly as to waste her time, when she ought to be putting in some good hard work preparing for the exam.

But, surprisingly enough, it was Connie who put her finger on the right spot! She had a great scorn for the weak ineffectual Gwendoline. She was a domineering, strong-minded girl herself, and she could not bear Gwendoline's moaning and grumbling. For some reason or other Connie had been touchy and irritable for the last week or two, and her bad temper suddenly flared out one evening at Gwen.

Gwendoline had come into the common room and flopped down in a chair. Everyone was swotting hard for the exam as usual, their heads bent over their books.

"I really must *not* carry heavy things again," began Gwendoline, in her peevish voice. Nobody took any notice except to frown.

"I've had to help Potty with the books in the library," went on Gwen. "Great heavy piles! It's set my heart fluttering like anything!"

"Shut up," said Connie. "We're working."

"Well, there's no need for you to be rude," said

111

Gwen, with dignity. "If you had a heart like mine
. . ."

And then Connie exploded. She got up and went
to stand over the astonished Gwendoline.

"You haven't *got* a heart, weak or otherwise! You're
a big bundle of pretence! You're making it all up to get
out of School Cert. *I* can see through you! That's why
you're not working, isn't it – because you're banking
on your heart letting you out, in some way or other
you've planned! Well, let me tell you this – I don't
care tuppence whether you do School Cert. or not, or
whether you work or not – but I *do* care about my own
work! And so do the others. So SHUT UP about your
silly heart, and keep away from us with your moanings
and groanings till School Cert. IS OVER!"

With that Connie went back to her seat, glowering.
Everyone was startled – too startled to say a word.
They all felt that what Connie said was true.

"You hateful, cruel thing!" said Gwendoline in a
trembling voice. "I hope you fail! And you will, too
– see if you don't! You only get decent marks because
you're always cribbing from Ruth. We all know that!
She'll pass and you won't! I think you're a beast!"

She burst into tears, got up and went out of the
room, banging the door so violently that Mam'zelle
and Miss Potts, working in their room not far away,
wondered whatever was happening.

The girls looked at one another. Alicia made a face.
"Well, I expect Connie's right – though you were a bit
brutal, weren't you, Connie?"

"No more brutal than you sometimes are," said
Connie, rather sulkily. "Anyway, let's go to work
again. Some of us are not like you, Alicia – skating
lightly over every subject and doing everything well,
without bothering. You don't understand how hard
some of us find our work. Let's get on."

112

There was silence in the room as the girls worked away, reading, making notes, learning by heart. Only Clarissa and Mary-Lou were really troubled about Gwen. Clarissa still believed in her weak heart, and Mary-Lou was always sorry for anyone who cried.

As for Gwendoline, her tears were not tears of sorrow, but of rage. That horrible Connie! If only she could get back at her for her unkind words. How Gwendoline hoped that Connie hadn't spoilt her beautiful plan!

Half term at Last

Half term came at last. It was a really lovely day, with bright sunshine and a nice breeze. The kitchen staff worked with a will to produce masses of good things for the grand School Tea. All the girls were excited about seeing their parents.

Gwendoline had quite thought that Clarissa's parents were coming, and had planned to introduce them to her mother and father. Then she suddenly heard Bill and Clarissa planning a picnic together on the half-term Saturday!

"Two of my brothers have their half term at the same time," said Bill, "so they're coming with Mother and Daddy. We'll take our lunch up to the top of Langley Hill, shall we, and bathe in the cove afterwards, before we come back to the Tennis Exhibition."

Gwen listened in astonishment. "But what will Clarissa's father and mother say to that?" she said.

"Won't they want Clarissa to themselves?"

"They can't come on the Saturday, worse luck," said Clarissa. "They may be able to come over on Sunday though – at least, Mother might be able to, even if Daddy can't. They're dreadfully busy people, you know."

"So I've asked Clarissa to come with us," said Bill. "My family will bring enough lunch for twice as many as we'll be, so we'll have a good time!"

Gwen was jealous. Why, she could have had Clarissa spend the day with *her*, if she'd known.

"Well! You might have told *me* your parents couldn't come on Saturday," she said. "You know how much I should have liked you to spend your time with *my* parents."

Clarissa looked embarrassed. She had purposely not told Gwen, because she had so much wanted to go with Bill and her brothers – all nice horsy people! But she couldn't explain that to Gwen. So, to make up for her remissness she was extra nice to her, and promised to go and speak to Gwen's people when they arrived.

"You might just *mention* my heart to them, said Gwendoline. "I don't really like to make a fuss about it myself – but *you* could just say something, Clarissa."

"Of course I will," said Clarissa, who still believed in Gwen's weak heart. "I think something ought to be done about it."

So, on half-term Saturday, Clarissa was led up to Mrs Lacy, Gwendoline's mother, and Miss Winter, her gentle and scared-looking old governess. Her father was not there.

Mrs Lacy was talking to another mother. Clarissa sat down on the grass with Gwendoline, waiting till she had finished. Darrell's mother was near, and Darrell introduced her to Clarissa.

Soon she heard Gwen talking to her mother and

Miss Winter. "Well, dear," said her mother, fondly, "and what has my darling Gwendoline been doing this term? Are you in the exhibition tennis?"

"Well, no, Mother," said Gwendoline. "I was almost chosen but it was decided only to have girls from the fifth and the sixth."

"How stupid!" said Miss Winter, feeling that Gwen would certainly have been better than any fifth- or sixth-form girl.

"What about your swimming, Gwen?" asked her mother. "You said in one of your letters that you had won a backstroke swimming race and I *did* think that was clever. Backstroke is *so* difficult. It remember I could never do it at school because the water kept going over my face."

Clarissa couldn't help hearing this conversation, though she was talking to Mrs Rivers, Darrell's mother. She was horrified. Whatever did Gwen mean by all this?

"No, I'm not swimming today," said Gwen. "There's a lot of jealousy, you know, Mother – often the good ones aren't given a proper chance. Still, I don't really mind. I can *dive* better than almost anyone now."

As Gwen always fell flat on her stomach, hitting the water with a terrific smack whenever she was made to dive, this was distinctly funny – or would have been to Darrell, Sally or Alicia. But it wasn't funny to Clarissa. It was shocking. What terrible lies – real thumping lies! However could Gwen say such things? Clarissa was very thankful that she was going out with blunt, straightforward Bill instead of having to be with Gwen and her silly, credulous mother. She saw very clearly why Gwen was as she was – this mother of hers had spoilt her, idolized her, believed every word she said – it was she – and probably that pathetic

115

little governess too – who had made Gwendoline into the silly, conceited, untrustworthy girl she was!

Clarissa felt that she really could *not* go and speak to Gwen's mother, after hearing all Gwen's untruths. She couldn't! Clarissa was meek, and weak in many ways, but she was straight and truthful. She was really shocked now.

She got up to slip away before Gwen could see she was going. But Gwen did see, and pulled her down again, so that she had to smile and say "How do you do?" to Gwen's mother and governess.

"I mustn't stop, I'm afraid," said Clarissa, hurriedly. "Bill's people have come and I mustn't keep them waiting."

Gwendoline looked at her meaningly. Clarissa knew what that look meant. "Say something about my heart." But alas, she found that she no longer believed in Gwendoline's heart. She was sure that the girl had lied about that now, just as she had lied about the other things a few minutes back.

"And are *you* in the tennis or swimming exhibitions?" asked Mrs Lacy, her large, pale blue eyes, so like Gwen's, looking down at Clarissa's small face.

"No, I'm not, I'm afraid," said Clarissa.

"You see, *poor* Clarissa has a weak heart," said Gwen, hastily, seeing a very good opening indeed here for Clarissa to bring up the subject of Gwen's own heart. But Clarissa didn't say a word.

"Poor child," said Mrs Lacy. "What a dreadful affliction for a young girl. Now Gwen has always had such a *strong* heart, I'm glad to say. And doesn't she look well now – so plump and bonny."

Gwen looked at Clarissa in desperation. This was all wrong! She gave her a sharp nudge. But still Clarissa didn't mention Gwen's weak heart! Gwen glared at her angrily.

116

Clarissa was now tongue-tied. She sat there, red in the face, her eyes blinking behind their thick glasses, wondering how in the world to get away from Gwen and her silly mother.

Bill came to her rescue with a shout. "Clarissa! I say, can you come? We're ready!"

"I must go," said Clarissa, nervously, and got up gladly. "Goodbye, Mrs Lacy."

"But, Clarissa!" called Gwendoline after her, dismayed and angry that Clarissa hadn't done what she had said she would do.

"*Who* did you say that girl was?" said Mrs Lacy. "I didn't catch the name."

"It's Clarissa Carter," said Gwen, sulkily. "Why did she have to rush off like that? Rude, I call it!"

"A most unattractive child," said Mrs Lacy. "Very plain indeed. No manners either. Gwendoline, I do hope she isn't a friend of yours."

"Oh *no*, Mother!" said Gwendoline, making up her mind that after Clarissa's failure to help her that morning she would never be friendly with her again! "I don't like her at all. Very plain, as you say – almost ugly – and undergrown, too. Not at all clever, and rather unpopular."

"I should think so!" said Miss Winter. "She must have been very badly brought up. When I compare her with Gwendoline – well!"

Gwendoline basked in their approval. She kept a sharp watch for Mam'zelle. Mam'zelle was her only hope now!

The day went by very fast. The tennis exhibition was loudly applauded, and the swimming and diving were exclaimed at in wonder, even the fathers admiring the crisp clean strokes of the fast swimmers, and the beautiful diving.

Afterwards the dancing display was held in the

amphitheatre of grass in the centre of the great courtyard. Mothers and fathers sat on the stone ledges surrounding the big circle, looking for their own girls as they came tripping in, dressed in floating tulle of different colours – and each parent, of course, felt certain that her own child was quite the nicest there!

Clarissa came back after her picnic lunch with Bill and her family. She did not go near Gwen, and would not even look in her direction in case she was beckoned over. But Gwen made no sign – she had finished with Clarissa, the horrid little two-faced thing.

Most unfortunately for Gwendoline, Mam'zelle kept quite out of reach the whole day. She was busy helping the dancing mistress, dressing the girls, arranging their tulle skirts and wings, thoroughly enjoying herself. Gwendoline had to comfort herself by thinking that she would find it easy to get Mam'zelle the next day. She would ask Mam'zelle to show her mother and Miss Winter the beautiful bedspread she was making. Mam'zelle would certainly love to do that – she was very proud of her bedspread!

"I wish this day wasn't over," sighed Darrell that night. "It was lovely – and what a smashing tea!"

She was happy because her mother and father hadn't said a word about her not being head girl any longer – but each of them had managed to convey to her that they understood all about it, and were backing her valiantly – her father by an extra hard hug, and her mother by linking her arm in Darrell's and holding it very hard as she walked round the Towers with her.

Felicity, of course, was mad with joy to see her parents again. "I love Malory Towers!" she kept saying. "Thank you for sending me here, Mummy and Daddy. I simply LOVE it!"

Before the Exam

The next day most of the girls expected their parents again, and could go out with them the whole day long. Clarissa stood at the window, looking out eagerly.

Gwendoline saw her. "I suppose she's looking for her mother," she thought. "Horrid thing. I shan't even speak to her!"

She saw Clarissa suddenly wave in delight. Then she ran from the room and disappeared down the stairs. Gwen looked out to see what Clarissa's mother was like – and if the car was a grand one.

To her surprise she saw an old Austin in the drive, and out of it stepped a most ordinary-looking woman. She had on a neat blue suit with a white blouse, and a scarf tied round her grey hair. She wore glasses, and had rather large feet in very sensible-looking shoes.

"Well! I don't think much of Clarissa's mother – *or* her car!" thought Gwen to herself. "Why, the car hasn't even been *cleaned*! And fancy arriving with a scarf tied round her head! My mother would never dream of doing that!"

She thought of her own mother with her large flowery hats, her flowery dresses, her flowery parasol, her floating scarves and strings of pearls. She would be ashamed of anyone like Clarissa's mother. She turned away, a sneer on her face, glad that she no longer meant to have Clarissa for a friend.

"What a *lovely* sneer!" said an aggravating voice,

and Gwen saw Belinda whipping out her pencil. "Hold it, Gwen, hold it!"

Gwen made a noise like a dog growling, and went out of the room. Now she must find Mam'zelle and tell her that her mother wanted to see the beautiful bedspread. This went down very well indeed, and Mam'zelle hurried to get it to show "that nice kind Mrs Lacy"!

Every single girl was out for the whole day, either with her own parents or with someone else's. Miss Grayling was glad that the half term came just before the School Certificate exam, so that the hard-worked girls might have a little time off to enjoy themselves. They really were working very hard, Miss Williams reported. Except Gwendoline Lacy, of course. *There* was an unsatisfactory girl for you!

By seven o'clock everyone was back – except Gwendoline!

"Where's our dear Gwendoline?" asked Alicia, looking round the supper table. Nobody knew. Then Mam'zelle, looking rather solemn, enlightened them.

"Poor Gwendoline – she has been taken home because of her bad heart," said Mam'zelle. "She has the palpitations so bad, poor, poor child. And will you believe it, when I told Mrs Lacy – ah, the poor woman – about Gwendoline's affliction, she said that the dear, brave child had not complained to her, or said a single word. *Vraiment*, this poor child is to be admired!"

The girls digested this startling information in astonishment. They looked at one another. "So Gwen's pulled it off after all," said Sally. "She'll miss the exam!"

Mam'zelle overheard. "Yes, she will miss the exam – and how upset she was. 'No, Mother,' she said, so bravely, 'I cannot go home with you – I must do the exam. I did not tell you of my trouble because I could

120

not bear to miss the exam!' That is what she said. With my own ears I heard her."

The Upper Fourth felt sick. What a sham! How hateful of Gwendoline to upset her mother like that! And she had got her way after all and would miss the exam. Clever, deceitful, sly Gwendoline!

"You were right, Connie," said Alicia. "*How* right! Mam'zelle, what's going to happen to our darling Gwendoline Mary then? Isn't she coming back this term? *That* would be too good to be true!"

"I don't know," said Mam'zelle. "I know nuzzing more. I am glad I was able to tell Mrs Lacy. Just to think that if I had not taken my bedspread to show her, she would never have known."

"I suppose *Gwen* asked you to take the bedspread?" said Connie. "And I suppose one of her palpitations came on whilst you were there, Mam'zelle?"

"I do not understand why you talk in this sneering way, Connie," said Mam'zelle, surprised. "You must not be hard. You must have sympathy."

The girls made various rude noises, which surprised Mam'zelle very much. Why these poohs and pahs and pullings of faces? No, no, that was not kind! Mam'zelle pursed up her lips and said no more.

"Well," said Darrell, in the dormy that night, "Gwen's got away with it all right – but fancy Mam'zelle falling for all that. Mam'zelle Rougier wouldn't. She sees right through Gwendoline – just like Miss Williams does!"

"All the same – she's lucky, getting out of the exam," groaned Belinda. "Wish *I* could! It's going to be awful to swot and swot all this week, after such a lovely half term. And then – next Monday the exam! I'm surprised you can't all hear my heart going down with a plop into my bedroom slippers!"

It was very hard to swot in such lovely weather.

Alicia longed for a game of tennis. Darrell longed for the swimming pool. Clarissa longed to go and laze in the flowery courtyard and watch the goldfish jumping. Belinda wanted to go out sketching. Irene became plagued with an enchanting tune that begged to be put down on paper – but poor Irene had to turn her back firmly on the lilting melody, and do pages and pages of French translation.

There was a lot of touchiness and irritability that week. The twins were on edge, especially Ruth, though she had less to fear in the exam than Connie, who was not nearly so well up to standard. Irene was touchy because she wanted to get at her beloved music and couldn't. Darrell was irritable because she was too hot. Mavis was hot and bothered because she thought she was going to have a sore throat – just as her voice seemed about to get right, too!

Only Alicia seemed really cheerful and don't-carish, and this attitude infuriated the others at times. Alicia was always the one to finish her work first and go off to swim. She could do her work and whistle an irritating little tune all the time, which nearly drove the others frantic. She laughed at their earnest faces, and their heartfelt groans.

"It's not worth all this amount of misery," she would say. "It's only School Cert. Cheer up, Connie – don't look like a dying duck over that French."

Connie flared up as she had done to Gwendoline. She banged her book down on the table and shouted. "Be quiet! Just because things are easy for you to learn, you sneer at others who aren't so lucky! Wait till you have a bad headache and have to learn pages of French poetry. Wait till your mind goes fuzzy because you're tired and want to sleep, and you know you mustn't. Wait till you have a bad night and have to think of things to say in a composition. Then you won't be quite so hard and don't-carish and sneering, and you'll shut up that awful whistling, too!"

Alicia was startled. She opened her mouth to retaliate, but Sally spoke first.

"Connie doesn't really mean all that," she said in her quiet calm voice. "We're all overworking and we're irritable and touchy. We'll be all right when the exam is over. After all, it's an important exam for us, and we're all taking it seriously and doing our best. Let's not squabble and quarrel when we want to save ourselves up for next week."

Darrell looked at Sally in admiration. How did she always know the right things to say? She had certainly poured oil on the troubled waters very successfully, because Connie spoke up at once.

"I'm sorry I said all that, Alicia. I *am* overworking and I'm touchy."

"It's all right," said Alicia, rather taken aback by this swift apology. "Sorry about my whistling – and if anyone wants any help, they've only got to ask me. I'll share these envied brains of mine with anyone!"

After this there was peace. Alicia shut her book quietly and crept out. The others worked on in silence. Would they ever, ever know all they ought to know for the exam? Why hadn't they swotted more during the year? Why hadn't they done this and that and the other! In fact their thoughts were almost exactly the same as every other exam-class's thoughts the week before the exam!

The week went by, and the girls worked more and more feverishly. Miss Williams forbade any work to be done on the Sunday before the exam, and there were deep groans.

And then came a surprise. Gwendoline arrived back at Malory Towers!

She came back on the Saturday, just before supper,

looking subdued and tearful. She had a short interview with Miss Grayling, and then was sent to join the others, who had just gone in to their supper.

"Why, GWEN!" said Mavis, in astonishment, seeing her first. "We thought you weren't coming back."

"Ah, here is Gwendoline back again," said Mam'zelle. "And how is the poor heart?"

"All right, thank you," mumbled Gwen, slipping into her seat, and trying to look as if she was not there.

The girls saw that she had been crying and tried not to look at her. They knew how horrid it was to have people looking at red eyes.

"Jolly lucky you'll be, next week," said Sally, trying to make light conversation. "Whilst we're all answering exam papers, you'll be lazing away in the courtyard, doing what you like!"

There was a little pause. "I've got to go in for the exam," said Gwen, in a choking voice. "That's why they've sent me back. It's too *bad*."

To the girls' dismay Gwendoline's tears began to fall fast into her plate of salad. They looked at one another uncomfortably. Whatever had happened?

"Better not say any more," whispered Darrell. "Don't take any notice of her. Poor Gwen!"

The Exam Week

Nobody ever knew what exactly had happened to Gwen. She was much too hurt and ashamed to tell anyone the story. So she said nothing, but went about subdued and red-eyed the whole weekend.

124

Everything had gone so well at first! Her frightened mother had taken her straight home, after Mam'zelle had mentioned Gwen's strange heart flutterings and palpitations. She had made her lie down and rest, and she and Miss Winter had fussed over her like a hen with one chick. Gwendoline had loved every minute, and had at once produced the languid ways and the feeble voice of the invalid.

She was rather pleased to know that her father was away and not likely to be back at all that week. By that time Gwen hoped she would be established as a semi-invalid, would miss all the exam, and might then gradually get better, once the exam danger was over.

The doctor came and listened solemnly to Gwen's mother's frightened explanations. "I'm *so* afraid it's her heart that's wrong, Doctor," she said. "The games are *very* strenuous at school, you know."

The doctor examined Gwen carefully. "Well, I can't find anything wrong," he said. "Nothing that a week's rest won't put right, anyway. She's a bit fat, isn't she – she could do with a bit of dieting, I should think."

"Oh, but Doctor – there *must* be something wrong with the child's heart," insisted Mrs Lacy. "Miss Winter and I have been very troubled to see how she loses her breath, and can hardly get up to the top stair when she goes to her bedroom."

"Well – why not get another opinion then?" said the doctor. "I should like you to satisfy yourself about Gwendoline."

"I'll take her to a specialist," said Mrs Lacy, at once. "Can you recommend one, Doctor?"

The doctor could and did, and on Wednesday the languid invalid was carefully driven up to London to see the recommended specialist. He took one quick glance at Gwendoline and sized her up at once.

He examined her very carefully indeed, with so

many "hm's" and "ha's" that Gwendoline began to feel frightened. Surely she hadn't *really* got something the matter with her? She would die if she had!

The specialist had a short talk with Mrs Lacy alone. "I will think over this, and will write to your doctor full details and let him know the result of my consideration. In the meantime, don't worry," he said.

On Friday the doctor got a letter from the specialist, and it made him smile. There was nothing wrong with Gwendoline's heart, of course, in fact nothing wrong anywhere at all, except that she was too fat, and needed very much more exercise. "Games, and more games, gym, walks, no rich food, no sweets, plenty of hard work, and no thinking about herself at all!" wrote the specialist. "She's just a little humbug! Swimming especially would be good for her. It would take some fat off her tummy!"

The doctor had to paraphrase all this considerably, of course, when he telephoned the news to Mrs Lacy that there was nothing the matter with Gwen. "I should send her back to school at once," he said. "It's not good for the girl to lie about like this."

Gwen was angry and miserable when she heard all this. She laid her hand to her heart as if it pained her. "Oh, Mother!" she said. "I'll go back if you say so – but give me one more week – I feel so much better for the rest."

Mrs Lacy promised Gwen that she should not go back for another week or more. Gwen was satisfied. So long as she missed the exam she didn't mind!

Then her father arrived home, anxious because of his wife's letters and telephone calls about Gwen. Gwen lay on the couch and gave him a pathetic smile. He kissed her, and inquired anxiously what the specialist had said.

"What! *Nothing* wrong," he said in astonishment. "I'll go round and see the doctor. I'd like to see the specialist's letter myself. I shall feel more satisfied then."

And so it came about that Gwen's father actually read the candid letter – saw that Gwen was called a "little humbug" – knew very clearly indeed that once more his daughter had tried a little deception – a cruel deception, that had caused her parents much anxiety – and all because she had merely wanted to get out of working for the exam.

What he said to Gwendoline the girl never forgot. He was angry and scornful and bitter – and at the end he was sad. "You are my only child," he said. "I want to love you and be proud of you like all parents. Why do you make it so hard for me to be proud of you, and to love you, Gwendoline? You have made your mother ill with this, and you have made me angry and disgusted – and very sad."

"I won't do it again," sobbed Gwendoline, terrified and ashamed.

"You must go back to school tomorrow," said her father.

"Oh no, Daddy! I can't! It's the exam," wailed Gwendoline. "I haven't done any work for it."

"I don't care. Go in for it just the same, fail and be humiliated," said her father. "You have brought it all on yourself. I am telephoning to Miss Grayling to apologize for taking you away, and to give her the specialist's instructions – games, more games, gym, walks – and most of all swimming!"

Swimming! The one thing Gwen detested most of all. She dissolved into tears again and wept the whole of the evening and the whole of the way down to Cornwall the next day. What had she done to herself? She hadn't been so clever after all! It had all ended in her having to take the exam without working for it, and in having to go in for games more than ever – and probably bathe every single day in that nasty cold pool! Poor Gwen. People do often bring punishment on themselves for foolishness – but not often to the extent that Gwendoline did.

The exam began. Everyone was jittery – even Alicia, curiously enough. Day after day the work went on, whilst the bright July sun shone in through the open windows, and the bees hummed enticingly outside. The girls were glad to rush off to the swimming pool after tea each day – then back again they went to swot up for the next day's exam.

Something curious had happened to Alicia. She didn't understand it. The first day she sat and looked at the questions, feeling sure they would be easy for her. So they were. But she found that she could not collect her thoughts properly. She put her hand up to her head. Surely she wasn't beginning a headache!

She struggled with the questions – yes, *struggled* – a thing the quick-witted, never-at-a-loss Alicia had hardly ever done before! She looked round at the others, puzzled – goodness, how could they write so quickly? What had happened to her?

Alicia had seldom known a day's illness. She was strong and healthy and clever. She really could not imagine why this exam was so difficult. She could not go to sleep at night, but lay tossing and turning. Had she been overworking? No – surely not – the others had worked far harder than she had, and had envied her for not having to swot so much. Well, WHAT was it then?

"Gosh," thought Alicia, trying to find a cool place on her pillow, "I know what it must feel like now, to have slow brains like Daphne, or a poor memory like Gwendoline. I can't remember a thing – and if I try, my brains won't work. They feel as if they want oiling!"

The others noticed that Alicia was rather quiet and subdued that week, but as they all felt rather like that, they said nothing. Quite a few of them went about looking very worried. Ruth looked white and drawn, Connie looked anxious, Gwendoline looked miserable, Daphne was almost in tears over the French – what a collection they were, thought Miss Williams – just like every other School Certificate form she had ever known, when exams were on. Never mind – it would be all behind them next week, and they would be in the highest spirits!

She glanced at one or two of the papers when they were collected. Darrell was doing fine! Gwendoline would be lucky if she got quarter marks! Mary-Lou was unexpectedly good. Connie's was poor – Ruth's was not good either. How strange! Ruth was usually well up to standard! It was doubtful if she would pass, if she completed the rest of her papers badly. And Alicia! Whatever in the world had happened to *her*! Bad writing – silly mistakes – good gracious, was Alicia playing the fool?

But Alicia wasn't. She couldn't help it. Something had happened to her that week and she was frightened now. "It must be a punishment to me for always laughing and sneering at people who aren't as quick and clever as I am," she thought, in dismay. "My brains have gone woolly and slow and stupid, like Gwen's and Daphne's. I can't remember a thing. How horrible! I'm trying so hard, too, that my head feels as if it's bursting. Is this what the others feel sometimes, when I laugh at them for looking so serious over their work? It's horrible, horrible, horrible! If only my brains would come back properly! I'm frightened!"

"Is anything the matter, Alicia?" said Darrell, on the last day of the exam. "You look all out."

Alicia never complained, no matter what went wrong with her. "No," she said. "I'm all right. It's just the exam."

She sat next to Darrell for the exam. At the end of the last paper, Darrell heard a slight noise. She looked up and gave a cry. Alicia had fallen forward over her papers!

"Miss Williams! Alicia's fainted!" she called. Matron was called, and as soon as Alicia came round again, looking bemused and strange, she was taken to the san. Matron undressed her – and cried out in surprise.

"You've got *measles*, Alicia! Just *look* at this rash – I never saw anything like it in my life! Didn't you notice it before?"

"Well – yes – but I thought it was just a heat rash," said Alicia, trying to smile. "Oh, Matron – I'm so glad it's only measles. I thought – I really thought my brains had gone this week. I felt as if I was going potty, and I was awfully frightened."

Alicia felt so thankful when she got in bed and rested her aching head against the cool pillow. She felt ill, but happy. It was only measles she had had that awful week! It wasn't that her brains had really gone woolly and stupid – it wasn't a punishment sent to her for sneering at the others who were slower than herself – it was just – measles.

And with that Alicia fell asleep and her temperature began to go down. She felt much better when she awoke. Her brains felt better, too!

"I'm afraid you'll have no visitors or company this week, Alicia," said Sister, who was in charge of the san. Matron had now departed back to school. "Just your own thoughts!"

Yes – just her own thoughts. Thankfulness that she wasn't going to be slow and stupid after all – shame that she had been so full of sneers and sarcastic remarks to others not so clever as herself – sadness because she knew she must have done terrible papers, and would surely fail. She would have to take School Cert. all over again! Blow!

"Well," thought Alicia, her brains really at work again, as her strong and healthy body began to throw off the disease, "well – I'd better learn my lesson – I shan't be so beastly hard again. But I honestly didn't know what it was like to have slow brains. Now I do. It's awful. Fancy having them all your life and knowing you can't alter them. I'll never sneer at others again. Never. At least, not if I can remember it. It's a frightful habit with me now!"

It was indeed. Alicia was going to find it very hard indeed to alter herself – but still, she had taken the first important step – she had realized that there was something to alter! She would never be quite so hard again.

The exams were over at last! The girls went quite mad and the mistresses let them! The swimming pool was noisy and full, the tennis courts were monopolized by the Upper Fourth, the kitchen staff were begged for ice-creams and iced lemondade at every hour of the day – or so it seemed! Girls went about singing, and even sour-faced Mam'zelle Rougier smiled to see them so happy after the exam.

Gwendoline wasn't very happy, of course. Miss Grayling had taken her father's instructions seriously, and Gwen was having more games, more walks – and more swimming than she had ever had before. But it was no good complaining or grumbling. She had brought it all on herself – it was nobody's fault but her own!

The Connie Affair

"Now we can have a good time for the rest of the term," said Darrell, pleased. "No more swotting – no more long preps even, because Miss Williams says we've done enough. We'll enjoy ourselves!"

"It ought to be a nice peaceful end of term, with no horrid happenings," said Sally. "When Alicia comes back, it will be nicer still."

Sally was wrong when she said there would be a nice peaceful end of term, with no horrid happenings – because the very next day the Connie Affair began.

It began with quite small things – a missing rubber – an essay spoilt because a page was missing, apparently torn out – a lace gone from one of Connie's shoes.

Nobody took any notice at first – things always *were* missing anyhow and turned up in the most ridiculous places – and pages did get torn out of books, and laces had a curious habit of disappearing.

But the Connie Affair didn't end there. Connie was always in trouble about something! "Now my French poetry book has gone!" she complained. "Now my cotton has gone out of my workbasket." Now this and now that!

"But, Connie – how is it that so many things happen to you lately?" said Darrell, puzzled. "I don't understand it. It's almost as if somebody was plaguing you – but who could it be? Not one of us would do silly, idiotic things like this – sort of first-form spite!"

Connie shook her head. "I can't think who's doing

it," she said. "I suppose it *is* someone. It can't be a series of accidents – there's too many of them."

"What do *you* think about it, Ruth?" asked Darrell – but Connie answered first.

"Oh, Ruth can't think who does it, either. It's very upsetting for her, because twins are always so fond of one another. She's sweet, too – keeps on giving me her things when I lose mine."

"Well, it's certainly most extraordinary," said Darrell. "I'm very sorry about it, it's a horrid thing to happen in the *fourth* form!"

The girls talked about the Connie Affair, as they called it, and puzzled about it. One or two of them looked at Gwendoline, wondering if she had anything to do with it.

"Don't you remember how Connie flared out at Gwen and put her finger on Gwen's weak spot – when she was putting over that nonsense about her heart?" said Daphne. "And you know – Gwen *has* done these nasty tricks before. Don't you remember? She did them to Mary-Lou when we were in the second form."

"Give a dog a bad name and hang him," quoted Darrell. "Just because Gwen did once do things like this, and got a bad name for it, doesn't mean we ought to accuse her of the same thing now. For goodness' sake wait a bit before we decide anything."

"There speaks a head girl," said Irene.

Darrell flushed. "I'm not head girl," she said. "Wish I was. But seriously, it really is jolly odd, all this business. The things are so very *silly* too – Connie's inkpot was stuffed up with blotting paper this morning, did you know?"

"Well!" said Belinda. "How petty!"

"Yes – most of the things are petty and spiteful and quite futile," said Darrell. "You don't suppose they'll

133

get any worse, do you? I mean – stop being petty and get harmful?"

"Let's hope not," said Mavis. "Here are the twins, Hallo, Connie – anything more to report?"

"Yes – somebody's cut my racket handle," she said, and showed it to them. "Just where I grip it! Mean, isn't it?"

"You can use mine, Connie. I told you," said Ruth, who was looking very distressed. "You can use anything of mine."

"I know, Ruth – but supposing your things get messed up, too?" said Connie. "I'd hate that."

"It's all very, very weird," said Irene, and hummed a new melody she had just composed. "Tooty-tooty-tee!"

Mavis sang to it – "Its all – very – weird! It's all – very – weird!"

"I say!" said Darrell. "Your voice is coming back! That's just how you *used* to sing, Mavis! It is, really."

"Yes, I know," said Mavis, her face red with pleasure. "I've tried it out when I've been alone – though that's not often here! – and *I* thought it had come back, too. Let me sing a song for you, and you can tell me if you think I've got my voice back!"

She sang a song that the lower school had been learning. "Who is Sylvia, what is she?" The girls listened spellbound. Yes – there was no doubt about it, Mavis's lovely low, powerful voice had come back again – better than ever. And this time it was owned by a Somebody, not a Nobody, as it had been before!

"We shall once again hear you saying, 'When I'm an opera singer and sing in Rome and New York and . . .' " began Darrell. But Mavis shook her head.

"No, you won't. You know you won't. I'm not like that now. Or am I? Do say I'm not!"

134

"You're not, you're not!" said everyone, anxious to reassure a girl they all liked.

Darrell clapped her on the back.

"I'm *so* glad, Mavis. That almost makes up for this horrid Connie Affair. You'll be able to have singing lessons again next term."

For a day or two it seemed as if the Connie Affair was at an end. Connie did not report any more strange happenings. Then she came to the common room almost in tears.

"Look!" she said, and held up her riding whip. It was one she had won at a jumping competition and was very, very proud of it.

The girls looked. Someone had gashed the whip all the way down, so that in places it was almost cut through. "I had it out riding this afternoon," said Connie, in a trembling voice. "I came home and took my horse to the stable . . ."

"You took two horses," said Bill. "Yours and Ruth's, too. I saw you."

"I took the horses to the stable," said Connie, "and left my whip there. When I went back to look for it, I found it like this!"

"Anyone in the stables?" said Darrell.

"No. Nobody at all. Bill had been there, of course, and June and Felicity had, too – and I and Ruth. Nobody else," said Connie.

"Well, *one* of those must have done it," said Darrell. "But honestly I can't believe any of them *did*. Ruth and Bill certainly wouldn't. My sister Felicity wouldn't even think of such a thing. And I feel pretty certain June wouldn't either, much as I dislike that cheeky little brat."

"Anyway, both the first-formers had gone by the time I'd stabled the horses," said Connie. "You didn't see them when we left, did you, Ruth?"

135

"No," said Ruth.

"Did you notice anyone else at *all*, when you were grooming your horse, Ruth?" asked Darrell, puzzled.

"She didn't even groom her horse," Connie answered for her. "I always do that. She stood there, looking at all the other horses, and would have seen anyone slinking round."

Everyone was puzzled. Ruth went out of the room and came back with her own whip, a very fine one. "You're to have this, Connie," she said. "I'm so upset about all these things happening. I insist on your taking my whip!"

"No, no," said Connie. "I don't mind taking things like rubbers and shoelaces – but not your beautiful whip."

That evening Darrell was alone with Bill. She was worried and puzzled. "Bill," she said, "are you *sure* there was nobody else in the stable but you and the twins this afternoon? I suppose – er – well, Gwendoline wasn't there, was she?"

"No," said Bill.

"I hated to ask that," said Darrell, "but it *is* just the kind of thing Gwen would do."

"It's her own fault if we think things like that of her," said Bill.

"Why does Connie groom Ruth's horse for her?" asked Darrell. "Is Ruth so lazy? She's always letting Connie do things!"

"No. She's not lazy," said Bill. "She's just odd, I think – a shadow of Connie! Well, I must go and give Thunder a lump of sugar, Darrell. See you later."

She went out and left Darrell thinking hard. A curious idea had come to her mind. She fitted one thing into another, like a jigsaw puzzle – she remembered all the unkind things that had been done to Connie, and she remembered also all the kind things that Ruth

136

had done to try and put right the unkind things. She remembered also a queer look she had seen on Ruth's face that evening, when Connie had refused Ruth's whip.

"A kind of frightened, half-angry look," thought Darrell. "Just as if she'd apologized to Connie, and the apology had been refused."

And then something clicked in her mind and she suddenly saw who the spiteful person might be that played all these petty tricks on Connie.

"What am I to do about it?" wondered Darrell. "I can't tell anyone in case I'm wrong. It's got to be stopped. And I'm half afraid of going and tackling anyone to get it stopped. But I must! It's serious."

She got up and went in search of Ruth. Yes, it was Ruth she wanted, and Ruth she must tackle!

Darrell puts things Right

Where was Ruth? She wasn't in the common room or the dormy or the classroom. Where could she be?

"Anyone seen Ruth?" asked Darrell, when she met any girls in her search. Nobody had. But at last a second-former said she thought she had seen Ruth going into the gardeners' shed by the stables.

Darrell sped off to look. She came to the shed, where the gardeners kept their tools, and stopped outside the door to try and think what she was to say.

As she stood there, she heard a curious sound. Somebody was certainly in the shed – and the sound

137

was like a kind of groan. Darrell pushed open the door quietly and looked in.

Ruth was there, right at the back, sitting on some sacks. In her hand she held the cut and broken riding whip, which she had obviously been trying to mend.

She didn't see Darrell at first. She put her hand over her face and made another sound – either a groan or a sob, Darrell didn't know which.

"Ruth," said Darrell, going up. "Ruth! What's the matter?"

Ruth leapt up in fright. When she saw it was Darrell she sat down on the sacks again, and turned her face away, still holding the broken whip.

"Ruth," said Darrell, going right up to the girl, "why did you spoil that lovely whip of Connie's?"

Ruth looked up quickly, amazement and dismay on her face. "What do you mean?" she said. "I didn't spoil it! Who said I did? Who said so? Did Connie?"

"No. Nobody said so. But I know you did," said Darrell. "And it was you who did all the other horrid things, wasn't it? – took this and that, hid things, and broke things, anything you could get hold of that belonged to Connie."

"Don't tell anyone," begged Ruth, clasping Darrell's hand tightly. "Please don't. I won't do it again, ever."

"But Ruth – why did you *do* it?" asked Darrell, very puzzled. "Anyone would think that you hated your twin!"

Ruth slapped the broken whip against the sacks. She looked sulky. "I do *hate* her!" she said. "I always have done – but oh, Darrell, I love her, too!"

Darrell listened to this in surprise. "But you can't love a person and hate them at the same time," she said, at last.

"You can," said Ruth, fiercely. "You *can*, Darrell.

138

I love Connie because she's my twin – and hate her because – because – oh, I can't tell you."

Darrell looked for a long time at Ruth's bent head, and saw the tears rolling off her cheeks. "I think I know why you hate Connie," she said at last. "Isn't it because she's so domineering – always answering for you, doing things for you that you'd rather do yourself – pushing herself in front of you – as if she was at least two years older?"

"Yes," said Ruth, rubbing her wet cheeks. "I never get a chance to say what *I* think. Connie always gets in first. Of course, I know she must have a better brain that I have, but . . ."

"She hasn't," said Darrell, at once. "Actually she ought to be in the lower fourth, not in the upper. I heard Miss Williams say so. They only put her with you in the upper class because you were twins, and your mother said you wouldn't like to be separated. Connie only keeps up with the form because you help her so much!"

There was a silence. Darrell thought about every-thing all over again. How very strange this was! Then a question arose in her mind and she asked Ruth at once.

"Ruth – why did you *suddenly* begin to be so beastly to Connie? You never were before, so far as I noticed. It all seemed quite sudden."

"I can't tell you," said Ruth. "But oh – I'm so miserable about it."

"Well, if *you* won't tell me, I shall go and ask Connie," said Darrell, getting up. "Something's gone awfully wrong, Ruth, and I don't know if I can put it right, but I'm going to have a jolly good try."

"Don't go to Connie," begged Ruth. "I don't want you to tell her it was me that was so beastly all the time. And oh, Darrell, I was so *sorry* for Connie, too, when I saw how upset she was at losing her things. It's dreadful to hate somebody and make them unhappy, and then to know you love them, and try to comfort them!"

"I suppose that's why you kept giving Connie your own things," said Darrell, sitting down on a tub. "Strange business, this! First you hate your twin and do something to upset her, like spoiling the riding whip she loved – and then you love her and are sorry – and come to give her your own riding whip! I could see you were upset when she didn't take it."

"Darrell – I *will* tell you why I hated Connie so much lately," said Ruth, suddenly, wiping her eyes with her hands. "I feel I've got to tell someone. Well – it was something awful."

"Whatever was it?" said Darrell, curiously.

"You see – Connie adores me, and likes to protect me and do everything for me," began Ruth. "And so far we have always been in the same class together. But Connie was afraid she would fail in School Cert. and felt sure I would pass."

"So you would," said Darrell. "And Connie would certainly fail!"

"Well – Connie thought that if she failed and I passed, I'd go up into the lower fifth next term, and she would have to stay down in the Upper Fourth and take the exam again another term," went on Ruth. "And that would mean she wouldn't be with me any more. So she asked me to do a bad paper, so that I would fail, too – and then we could still be together!"

Darrell was so astonished at this extraordinary statement that she couldn't say a single word. At last she found her tongue.

"*Ruth*! how wicked! To make you fail and feel humiliated when you could so easily pass! She *can't* love you."

140

"Oh, but she does – too much!" said Ruth. "Anyway, I said I *would* do a bad paper – somehow I just can't help doing what Connie wants, even if it's something horrid like that – so I *did* do a bad paper – and then afterwards I hated Connie so much for making me do it that I did all these horrible things to her!"

Poor Ruth put her face in her hands and began to sob. Darrell went and sat on the sacks beside her and put her strong comforting arm round Ruth's shoulders.

"I see," she said. "It's all very peculiar and extraordinary, but somehow quite understandable. It's because you're twins, I expect. Connie should have been your elder sister, then it wouldn't have mattered! You could have loved each other like ordinary sisters do, and you'd have been in different forms, and things would have been all right. Cheer up, Ruth. It's all been frightening and horrible for you, but honestly I can see quite well how it all happened."

Ruth looked up, comforted by Darrell's simple explanation. She pushed her hair back and sniffed.

"Darrell, please, please don't tell Connie I did all those things," she said. "I'm awfully sorry now that I did. She wouldn't understand, and she'd be awfully upset and unhappy. I couldn't bear that."

"Yes – but you can't go on like this – being bossed by Connie, and being just an echo for her," said Darrell, sensibly. "I don't see any way of stopping it except for us to tell her. I'll come with you if you like."

But Ruth began to sob so much when Darrell suggested this that Darrell had to give up the idea. A distant bell sounded and she got up. "You'd better go and bathe your eyes," she said kindly. "I'll try and think of some way to put things right without telling Connie – but it's going to be difficult!"

Ruth went off, sniffing, but much comforted.

Darrell rubbed her nose hard, as she often did when she was puzzled. "There's only one thing to do!" she said. "And that's to tell Miss Williams. *Something's* got to be done!"

So that evening, after supper, Miss Williams was astonished to find Darrell at her door, asking for an interview. She wondered if Darrell had come to beg to have her position as head girl restored to her. But it wasn't that.

Darrell poured out the strange story of the twins. Miss Williams listened in the greatest amazement. The things that could go on in a school that nobody knew about, even though the girls concerned were under her nose all day long!

"So, you see, Miss Williams," finished Darrell, "if Ruth can't bear Connie to be told, everything is as bad as before! They'll both fail the exam, they'll both stay down in the Upper Fourth, instead of going up next term, and poor Ruth will go on being domineered over, and will hate and love Connie at the same time. It must be horrible."

"Very horrible," thought Miss Williams, horrified. "And very dangerous. Things like this often lead to something very serious later on." She did not say this to Darrell, who sat earnestly watching her, waiting for some advice.

"Darrell, I think it was very clever of you to find this out," said Miss Williams, at last. "And you have acted very wisely all through. I do really feel very pleased with you."

Darrell went red and looked pleased. "Can you think how to put things right?" she asked. "Oh, Miss Williams, *wasn't* it a pity that Ruth did a bad exam paper! If she hadn't things would have got right of themselves – the twins would have been in different forms."

"Darrell," said Miss Williams after a pause, "what I am going to say now is between you and me. I glanced at all the exam papers before sending them up – and Ruth didn't do quite as bad a one as she thought! In fact, I feel pretty certain she will scrape through."

"Oh *good*!" said Darrell, delighted. "I never thought of that. So they'll be in different forms next term after all, then!"

"I think so," said Miss Williams. "That will give Ruth a chance to stand on her own feet and develop a personality of her own, instead of being Connie's shadow – and Connie will have to stop domineering over her – it will all disappear naturally and gradually, which is the best thing that could happen, in this curious case."

"Won't Connie know anything then?" asked Darrell. "Won't she have to be told?"

"That will be Ruth's business, and no concern of anyone else's," said Miss Williams. "Some day, when the right time comes, she may choose to confess to Connie – and perhaps they will even laugh at it all. Keep an eye on Ruth for me, will you, Darrell, for the rest of the term? You're in her confidence now and I shall trust you to see that nothing else goes wrong between the twins."

"Oh, I will," said Darrell, pleased to be asked this. "I'd love to. I like Ruth."

"And Darrell – I shall make you head girl again in two days' time," said Miss Williams. "And this time I shall be very, very proud of you!"

Everyone was delighted when Miss Williams announced in her quiet voice, two days later, that Darrell was once more to be head girl of the form. "Thank you for taking on the position temporarily," she said to Sally. "But I am now convinced that Darrell deserves to be promoted again."

"Why, Darrell? Why has Miss Williams put you back as head this week?" asked Belinda and the others, after class. But Darrell didn't tell them, of course. Miss Williams hadn't actually said that it was because of her trying to put right the affair of the twins – but she knew that it was. She had really acted like a responsible head girl then.

No more spiteful things were done to Connie, and gradually the Connie Affair, as it was called, was forgotten. Ruth seemed to forget her dislike and resentment, and was very sweet to Connie. "Next term," thought Darrell, "things will be quite all right – they'll be in different forms, and Ruth can go ahead with her good brains, and Connie can work at her own pace and keep her hands off Ruth."

The term was slipping away fast now. Alicia was better, and fortunately no one else had caught measles from her. Most of the Upper Fourth had already had them, which was fortunate. Alicia groaned because she felt sure that she had failed – and would have to take the School Certificate all over again. She was to come back to school a week before Breaking-up. The girls were very pleased. They had all missed Alicia's quickness and sense of fun. Gwendoline was perhaps the only one who didn't want her back. Poor Gwen – she had already lost some of her fat, through having to play so much tennis and go for so many walks, and swim – or try to – each day! But she certainly looked healthier, and her spots were rapidly going.

Clarissa amazed the class one day by coming back from a visit to the dentist and the occulist looking completely different! "And that awful wire's been taken from my front teeth. Do you recognize me, girls?"

"Hardly!" said Darrell, and Belinda got out her pencil to make a sketch of this different and most attractive Clarissa!

She stood laughing in front of them – her deep green eyes flashing round, and her white teeth no longer spoilt by an ugly wire. Her wavy auburn hair suited her eyes, and she looked unusual and somehow distinguished.

"You'll be a beauty one day, Clarissa," said Belinda, her artist's eye seeing Clarissa at twenty-one, lovely and unusual in her colouring. "Well, well – talk about an ugly duckling turned into a swan!"

Clarissa was now fast friends with Bill, much to the girls' amusement. Nobody had ever thought that the boyish Bill, who seemed only to care for her horse Thunder, and for Miss Peters (but a good way behind Thunder!) would make a friend in her form. But she had, and the two chattered continually together, always about horses, and rode whenever they could. Gwendoline didn't care. Since she had seen Clarissa going off at half term with the dowdy-looking elderly woman in the old Austin car, she had taken no further interest in her.

Gwendoline wanted a grand friend, not somebody

ordinary, whose parents didn't even clean their old car when they came at half term! So Gwen was once more alone, with no one to talk or giggle with, no one to call her friend.

"We ought to do something to celebrate Alicia coming back," said Belinda. "She's coming tomorrow."

"Yes! Let's do something," said Darrell, at once.

"Something mad and bad," said Betty, who was in the courtyard with the others.

"A trick!" said Irene. "We haven't played a trick for two whole terms. Think of it! What are we coming to? We must be getting old and staid."

"Yes, let's play a trick," said Sally. "After all, the exams are over, and we worked jolly hard – we deserve a really good laugh!"

"What trick shall we play?" asked Mavis. "Betty, didn't you bring anything back this term? Last term you brought back that awful spider that could dangle from the ceiling like a real one – but we never got a chance of using it. Gosh, I'd like to have seen Mam'zelle's face if we had managed to let it down over her desk!"

Everyone giggled. "I didn't bring it back with me this term," said Betty, regretfully. "I stayed with Alicia in the hols and one of her brothers bagged it. But I tell you what I *have* got!"

"What?" asked everyone, getting thrilled.

"I haven't tried them yet," said Betty. "They're awfully strange things. They're little grey pellets, quite flat. One side is sticky, and you stick it to the ceiling."

"What happens?" asked Irene.

"You have to dab each pellet with some kind of liquid," said Betty, trying to remember. "At least, I *think* that's right – and then, according to the instructions, a little bubble detaches itself slowly from the pellet,

146

floats downwards, and suddenly pops – and makes a pinging sound."

Everyone listened in delight. "*Betty*! It's too marvellous for words!" said Irene, thrilled. "Let's play the trick tomorrow, to celebrate Alicia's coming back. We'll have to get the stepladder to put some of the pellets on the ceiling. Let's do it when Mam'zelle takes us. She's always fun to play tricks on."

So, with much secrecy, the stepladder was hidden in the cupboard outside the Upper Fourth classroom, and just before morning school, three flat grey pellets were quickly fixed to the ceiling, where, quite miraculously, so it seemed to the girls, they stuck very tightly indeed, and could hardly be seen at all.

Betty brushed each one over quickly with the liquid from a small bottle sent with the pellets. Then the ladder was bundled into the cupboard again, just as Mam'zelle's high heels were heard tip-tapping down the corridor. Daphne flew to hold the door open, and the others stood ready in their places.

"Merci, Daphne," said Mam'zelle, briskly. "Ah, Alicia – it is very, very good to see you back. You have had a bad time with your measle?"

"Well, actually I didn't mind my measle very much, after the first day," said Alicia, with a grin. She was looking very well now.

"It is good that no one got the measle from you," said Mam'zelle, sitting down at her desk.

"I had a measle last year," said Irene, and this was the signal for everyone to talk about when they had a measle, too. Mam'zelle had to bring the talk to an end, because it showed signs of getting very boisterous.

"We will have no more measly talk," she said, firmly, and wondered why the girls laughed so much at this.

They took quick, surreptitious glances at the ceiling

148

every now and again, longing to see the new trick at work. Alicia had heard all about it, of course, and was thrilled with their novel way of celebrating her return. She had suggested that everyone should pretend they could not see the bubbles, or hear the "ping" when they exploded.

"Mam'zelle will think she's gone crackers," she said. "I know I should if I saw bubbles that pinged round me when nobody else did!"

"Today I go through the questions that you answered on the exam paper," said Mam'zelle, smiling round. "You will tell me what you put and I will say if it was good or no."

"Oh *no*, Mam'zelle," protested Alicia. "We had to do the exam – let's forget it now it's over. Anyway, I did such a frightful paper, I've failed, I know. I can't bear to think of the exam questions now."

Irene nudged Belinda. One of the grey pellets was beginning its performance. A small grey bubble was starting to form up on the ceiling. It grew a little bigger, became heavy enough to detach itself, and floated gently down into the air. All three pellets had been placed just above the big desk belonging to Miss Williams, where Mam'zelle was now sitting.

With bated breath the girls watched the bubble slowly descend. It looked as if it was about to fall on Mam'zelle's head, decided not to, and skirted round her hair, near her left ear. When it got there, it burst suddenly, and a curiously sharp, very metallic "ping" sounded.

Mam'zelle almost jumped out of her skin. "*Tiens!*" she said "*Qu'est-ce que c'est que ça!* What was that?"

"What was what, Mam'zelle?" asked Sally innocently.

"A ping – *comme ça!*" said Mam'zelle, and pinged again. "Ping! Did you not hear a ping, Sally?"

149

"A ping? What exactly do you mean, Mam'zelle?" asked Sally, putting on a puzzled look that made Darrell want to cry with laughter. "You don't mean a *pong*, do you?"

"Perhaps she means a ping-pong," suggested Irene, and began to giggle. So did Mavis. Darrell frowned at them.

"I sit here and suddenly in my ear there comes a *ping!*" said Mam'zelle. "I feel it on my ear."

"Oh, I thought you meant you *heard* it," said Sally.

"I hear it and I feel it," said Mam'zelle. "*Que c'est drôle, ça!* How peculiar!"

Another bubble was now descending. The girls, trying not to appear as if they were watching it, waited for it to descend near Mam'zelle. It floated down and exploded behind her head. "Ping!" It was a most extraordinary little sound, small but very sharp and clear.

Mam'zelle leapt to her feet wildly. She turned and looked behind her. "There it comes again!" she cried. "It was on my neck – and ping! it went. What can this be?"

"I expect it's just noises in your ears, Mam'zelle," said Darrell, comfortingly. This made Irene give one of her terrific snorts, and Daphne and Mavis began to laugh helplessly.

"Do you not hear this 'ping', Darrell?" said Mam'zelle, beginning to look scared. "I am . . ."

"Ping!" Another bubble popped with a ping, and Mam'zelle stood with her mouth open in amazement. What was this pinging? And why could not the girls hear it? Aha – was it a trick?

"Is this a trick?" she began. "A bad, wicked trick on your poor old Mam'zelle again? I have not . . ."

Ping! A little bubble landed fairly and squarely on Mam'zelle's bun of hair on the top of her head and pinged valiantly. Mam'zelle shrieked.

"What is it?" she cried. "Stop laughing, girls! Tell me what it is, this ping."

She saw Irene looking up at the ceiling and she looked, too. But at that moment no bubble was descending, and she saw nothing. Then a bubble which had actually got almost to the floor without popping, pinged just by her foot. Mam'zelle jumped as if she had been shot. She leapt up again and made for the door.

"*C'est épouvantable!*" she cried. "It is unbelievable. I go to fetch help!"

Last Week of Term

By this time, of course, the girls were almost helpless with laughter. Tears were pouring down Darrell's cheeks and Sally was holding her sides, aching with laughter. Irene appeared to be choking and Alicia and Betty were holding on to each other helplessly.

Mam'zelle rushed to Miss Williams. She was taking a class in the second form, and was amazed at Mam'zelle's sudden entrance.

"Miss Williams! I beg you to come with me to your classroom," Mam'zelle besought the astonished Miss Williams. "It goes 'ping' and it goes 'pong' – right in my ears – yes, and down by my foot."

Miss Williams looked astounded. Was Mam'zelle off her head? What was all this ping and pong business? The second form began to giggle.

"Mam'zelle, what exactly do you mean?" asked Miss Williams, rather crossly. "Be more explicit."

151

"In your classroom there are pings and pongs," said Mam'zelle again. "The girls do not hear them, but I do. And I, I do not like it. Miss Williams, come, *je vous prie!*"

As it looked as if Mam'zelle was about to go down to her knees, Miss Williams got up hurriedly and went with her to the Upper Fourth. The girls had recovered a little and were on the watch to see who might be coming. One or two more bubbles had floated down and burst with sharp pings, and another was just about to descend.

"Sssst! It's Miss Williams," said Mavis, suddenly, from the door. "Straighten your faces."

With difficulty the girls pulled their faces straight, and stood up as Miss Williams entered with Mam'zelle.

"What is all this?" asked Miss Williams, impatiently. "What is it that Mam'zelle is complaining of? I can't make head or tail of it."

"It is a ping," wailed Mam'zelle, beginning to despair of making Miss Williams understand.

"I think Mam'zelle has noises in her ears," said Alicia, politely. "She hears pings and pongs, she says."

A bubble fell near Mam'zelle and burst. "Ping!"

Mam'zelle jumped violently and dug Miss Williams unexpectedly in the ribs with her finger. "There it comes again. Ping, it said!"

"Don't poke me like that, Mam'zelle," said Miss Williams, coldly, whereupon another bubble burst, and yet another, and two pings sounded almost together. Miss Williams began to look puzzled.

"I go," said Mam'zelle, and took a step towards the door. "I go. There is something ABOMINABLE in this room!"

Miss Williams firmly pulled Mam'zelle back. "Mam'zelle, be sensible. I heard the noise, too.

152

I cannot imagine why the girls do not hear it."

The girls suddenly decided they had better hear the next ping – so, when it came, they all called out together.

"Ping! I heard it, I heard it!"

"Silence," said Miss Williams, and the girls stopped at once – just in time for a bubble to descend on Mam'zelle's nose and explode with an extra loud ping.

Mam'zelle shrieked. "It was a bobble! I saw a bobble and it went ping."

Miss Williams began to think that Mam'zelle really must be mad this morning. What was this "bobble" now?

And then Miss Williams herself saw a "bobble" as Mam'zelle called it. The bubble sailed right past her nose, and she gasped. It pinged beautifully on the desk and disappeared.

Miss Williams looked silently up at the ceiling. Her sharp eyes saw the three flat pellets there – and saw a bubble forming slowly on one. She looked back at the class, which, trying not to laugh, but not succeeding very well, gazed back innocently at her.

Miss Williams' lips twitched. She didn't know what the girls had done, nor exactly what the trick consisted of – but she couldn't help feeling that it was very ingenious – yes, and very funny, too, especially when played on someone like poor Mam'zelle Dupont, who could always be relied on to take fright at anything unusual.

"Mam'zelle, take your class out into the courtyard to finish the lesson," she said. "There will be no pings there. And if I were you I would give the housemaid instructions to take a broom and sweep the ceiling before you next take a class in this room."

This last suggestion reduced Mam'zelle to a state of such astonishment that she could only stand and stare after Miss Williams' departing figure. Sweep the *ceiling*! Was Miss Williams in her right mind?

The class began to giggle again at Mam'zelle's astounded face – and then as another ping sounded Mam'zelle plunged for the door. "*Allons-y,*" she said. "We have been much disturbed. We go to the courtyard! Come now, we will leave behind these bad pings and pongs and go to do some work."

The story of the pellets and their pings flew through the school and made every girl gasp and laugh. There were so many visitors to the Upper Fourth form room that Miss Williams grew quite cross.

She stood a broom by the door. "Anyone else who comes can sweep the ceiling six times," she said. "And let me tell you, it's not as easy as it looks!"

"Oh – that *has* done me good," said Alicia that night. "I've never laughed so much in my life. Mam'zelle's face when that first bubble pinged! I nearly died!"

"Miss Williams was rather a sport about it, wasn't she?" said Darrell. "She spotted the trick all right, and wanted to laugh. I saw her lips twitching. I'll be sorry to leave her form and go into the fifth."

"Yes – next term most of us will be up in the fifth," said Sally. "Goodness, how odd it will seem to be so far up the school."

"I've liked this term," said Darrell, "although it had its horrid bits – like when I lost my place as head girl."

"I was glad when you got it back again," said Ruth, speaking suddenly on her own, as she had done several times lately. She looked affectionately at Darrell. She had had a great admiration for her ever since Darrell had put things right for her – and had not told Connie. Miss Williams had quite casually told Ruth that although she had been disappointed in her exam paper, she thought probably she had passed all right – and that if Connie didn't, she hoped Ruth wouldn't very much mind her twin being left down in the fourth, whilst she, Ruth, went up into the fifth.

So it looked as if things would be better next term. Connie would soon get over the separation, and, after all, they would continually see each other in the dormy and at meal times.

The last few days of the term flew by. The Breaking-Up day seemed to come all at once. The usual pandemonium broke out. Mistresses began to feel as if they were slowly going mad as girls whirled past them, shouting and calling, and trunks were hurled about, night cases lost, rackets strewn all over the place, and an incessant noise raged in every tower.

The train girls went off first, and were loudly cheered as the coaches moved off down the drive. "Write to us! See you next term! Be good if you can! Hurrah!"

Darrell went to find Felicity, who seemed to be continually disappearing. She found her exchanging addresses with Susan. June had gone with the train-girls, and Darrell had noticed that Felicity had not even bothered to wave goodbye to her. So *that* friendship was finished with. Good! Darrell still thought of June with dislike, but now that her little sister was no longer dragged around by June, but was standing on her own feet, she had lost the desire to slap June hard!

"Felicity! As soon as I find you and stand you by the front door, you disappear again," said Darrell. "Daddy will be here soon with the car. For goodness' sake come with me and don't leave me again. Where's your bowler hat? You've got to take it home with you in case you go riding in the hols."

"It was here a minute ago," said Felicity, looking round. "Oh no, look – that pest of a Katie has got it – what an ass she looks – her head's miles too big for it. Katie! KATIE! Give me my BOWLER!"

"Felicity! Is there any *need* to yell like that?" said Miss Potts as she hurried by, almost deafened.

"Oh, Potty, I haven't said goodbye to you, Potty!" yelled Felicity. Darrell felt quite shocked to hear Felicity call her form mistress Potty.

"Felicity!" she said. "Don't call her that."

"Well! You told me that everyone was allowed to on the last day of term," said Felicity. "POTTY!"

Belinda came by with Irene's music case. "Anyone seen Irene? She wants her music case and I've just found it."

She disappeared and Irene came along, groaning. "Where's my wretched music? I put it down for a moment and some idiot has gone off with it."

"Belinda's got it. Hey, Belinda, BELINDA!"

Mam'zelle came walking by with her fingers in her ears and an agonized expression on her face. "These girls! They have gone mad! I am in an asylum. Why do I teach mad girls? Oh this noise, it goes through my head."

"Mam'zelle! MAM'ZELLE! Goodbye. My car's come."

"*Au revoir*, Mam'zelle. I say, is she deaf?"

"Hurrah! There's our car. Come on, Irene."

Clarissa came by, excitement making her green eyes gleam. She looked very pretty. "Mother's come," she shouted to Bill. "Come and see her. She wants to know if you can come and stay with me in the hols. Bill, come and meet my mother!"

Gwendoline went out at the same time as Bill and Clarissa. Drawn up by the great flight of steps was a magnificent Bentley, gleaming and shining. Leaning out was a charming auburn-haired woman, beautifully dressed. A most distinguished-looking man sat beside her.

"Mother!" shrieked Clarissa. "You've come at last. This is Bill. You said you'd ask her to stay in the hols!"

Gwendoline gaped in amazement to see this gleaming car, and such parents – parents to be really proud of! But – how could they be Clarissa's? Hadn't Gwen seen her dowdy grey-haired mother come and fetch her that Sunday at half term, in an old Austin car?

"Goodbye, Gwen," said Clarissa, seeing her standing near, but she did not offer to introduce the girl to her mother.

"I thought that was your mother who came to take you out at half term," said Gwen, unable to stop herself from looking surprised.

"Oh no – that was my dear old governess," said Clarissa, getting into the car. "Mother couldn't come, so Miss Cherry popped over in her old car to take me out instead. Fancy thinking she was my *mother*!"

Gwen's car was just behind, and Mrs Lacy was looking out and waving.

"Gwen! How are you? Oh, you *do* look well! Who was that pretty, attractive child that just went away in that beautiful Bentley? Is she in your form?"

"Yes," said Gwen, kissing her mother.

"Oh, I *do* hope she is a friend of yours," said her mother. "Just the kind of girl I'd like."

"You saw her at half term," said Gwen, sulkily. "And you *didn't* like her. That's Clarissa Carter."

Darrell and Felicity looked at each other and giggled. How sorry Gwen must be that she didn't get Clarissa's friendship! As it was, it was Bill who was going to spend most of the holidays with Clarissa, and not Gwen. Poor Gwen as usual wouldn't be asked anywhere.

"There's our car!" cried Felicity suddenly. She

157

caught Mam'zelle round the waist. "Goodbye, dear Mam'zelle. See you next term!"

"Ah, dear child!" said Mam'zelle, quite overcome at Felicity's sudden hug. She kissed her soundly on each cheek and everyone grinned at Felicity's startled expression.

"Goodbye!" cried Darrell, waving to the rest of the girls. "See you in September. Look out, Belinda, you're treading on somebody's bowler!"

"It's mine, it's mine," shrieked Felicity, in anguish. "Take your great foot off it, Belinda."

"You teach your young sister to be polite to her elders!" called Belinda, as Darrell and Felicity went headlong down the steps, almost knocking over poor Matron.

"Goodbye, Matron! Goodbye, Miss Williams! Goodbye, Potty! Hallo, Mother! Daddy, you look fine! Hurrah, hurrah, it's the holidays!"

And into the car piled the two girls, shouting, laughing, happy and completely mad. They leaned out of the window.

"Goodbye! Happy hols! See you soon again! Good old Malory Towers – we'll come back in September!"

Stories of Mystery and Adventure by Enid Blyton
in Armada

Mystery Series

Secrets Series

ARMADA

All these books are available at your local bookshop or newsagent, or can be ordered from the publisher. To order direct from the publishers just tick the title you want and fill in the form below:

Name _____

Address _____

_____

Send to: Collins Childrens Cash Sales
          PO Box 11
          Falmouth
          Cornwall
          TR10 9EN

Please enclose a cheque or postal order or debit my Visa/ Access –

   Credit card no:

   Expiry date:

   Signature:

– to the value of the cover price plus:

UK: 60p for the first book, 25p for the second book, plus 15p per copy for each additional book ordered to a maximum charge of £1.90.

BFPO: 60p for the first book, 25p for the second book plus 15p per copy for the next 7 books, thereafter 9p per book.

Overseas and Eire: £1.25 for the first book, 75p for the second book. Thereafter 28p per book.

ARMADA